I0571364

PRAISE FOR

KRISTINE KATHRYN RUSCH

"Rusch's greatest strength…is her ability to close down a story and leave the reader feeling that the author could not possibly have wrung any more satisfaction out of the piece."

—*The Kansas City Star*

"Rusch is a great storyteller—easily the equal of Patterson or Koontz."

—*Analog*

PRAISE FOR

A DANGEROUS ROAD: A SMOKEY DALTON NOVEL

(WRITING AS KRIS NELSCOTT)

"Nelscott has an absorbing story to tell, and she does it justice."

—*Philadelphia Inquirer*

"More than just offering a puzzle, this novel encourages self-examination about identity, responsibility and the consequences of choices. Smokey proves himself a man of conscience able to make tough choices. His return will be cause for celebration."

—*Publisher's Weekly*

"It's not hard to draw parallels between Nelscott's PI Smokey Dalton and Walter Mosley's Easy Rawlins, another secretive, canny black man trying to solve mysteries while circumspectly navigating the white world. But Dalton's no knock-off. (Would you label the hundreds of hard-boiled detectives who've appeared in Raymond Chandler's wake mere Marlow Xeroxes because they're white?)"

—*Entertainment Weekly*

Also by
Kristine Kathryn Rusch

The Sweet Young Things Mystery Series:

Spree
"Sweet Young Things"
"Christmas Eve at the Exit"

The Smokey Dalton Series (as Kris Nelscott):

A Dangerous Road
Smoke-Filled Rooms
Thin Walls
Stone Cribs
War at Home
Days of Rage
Street Justice

SPREE

A SWEET YOUNG THINGS MYSTERY

KRISTINE KATHRYN RUSCH

Spree

Copyright © 2015 by Kristine Kathryn Rusch

All rights reserved

Published 2015 by WMG Publishing
www.wmgpublishing.com
Cover and Layout copyright © 2015 by WMG Publishing
Cover design by Allyson Longueira/WMG Publishing
Cover art copyright © Carloscastilla/Dreamstime
ISBN-13: 978-0-615-80260-2
ISBN-10: 0-615-80260-5

*This book is licensed for your personal enjoyment only. All rights reserved.
This is a work of fiction. All characters and events portrayed in this book
are fictional, and any resemblance to real people or incidents is purely
coincidental. This book, or parts thereof, may not be reproduced
in any form without permission.*

SPREE

A SWEET YOUNG THINGS MYSTERY

— 1 —

Sunlight glinted off the highway, creating snow blindness in the middle of the summer desert. Moira wished she had sunglasses. She wished she had a thousand things, but as her last foster mother used to say, wishing didn't make it so.

Her arms ached from fighting the ancient minivan's steering wheel. A huge wind had been whipping her from Fallon—maybe before—and more than once she thought the entire vehicle would go over sideways.

Part of her cursed Royce Gallagher for tying the mattress onto the roof with only one bungee cord. A trucker had helped her pull another bungee across the top somewhere near Salt Lake when he saw her standing on the van's bumper and shoving.

Hon, you're gonna kill someone with that thing, he'd said as gently as he could. *I saw you on 80 and I was thinking the worst thing could happen is that could come loose.*

He reeked of cigarettes and diesel. She'd kept an eye on him the entire time, and she hadn't mentioned Kasey, sound asleep in the back seat. When he'd peered in, reaching among the boxes for a rope she swore was there, she'd nearly pushed him away.

But he'd helped and given her the bungee besides, and it had lasted for the next 500 miles, all the way here, Highway 95 in the most godforsaken place on Planet Earth.

The Nevada desert.

Holy Christ on a crutch. How did she get here?

The road wound for the first time in miles. Ahead, that flash of sun on the highway made it almost impossible to see. The signs—*Falling Rocks Ahead*—registered on her consciousness just after she passed them, her mouth dry, her face so hot it felt like she was going to burst from within.

Her air conditioning had broken in Nebraska. The gas station attendant sent her to a local mechanic who told her it would take two days to order the parts and nearly five hundred in labor.

Plus, he'd said, *you'll probably want to replace the belts and all the filters. This thing needs a good tuning, lady, and I can't guarantee we won't find something else. How long has it been since it's been serviced?*

She had no idea, so she lied. She said two years, and he about burst a gasket. *Two years? Lady, this thing is a death trap.*

She knew that. But she didn't have the cash to fix this thing, not that she wanted to. She batted her eyes at him, and he jury-rigged the air conditioning so that it cooled enough to keep them alive, and he replaced the filters. She paid him two hundred dollars out of her stash and he threw in some chocolate for Kasey.

Not that she needed chocolate. She ate too many sweets as it was.

Moira looked over her shoulder. Kasey was awake, strapped into the booster seat, bouncing her battered Barbie along her legs as if the doll had springs on her feet.

The last of the sunscreen went to Kasey. Her skin was even fairer than Moira's. Her white-blond hair made her look like a wisp, something that could vanish in a heartbeat.

"I'm hot," Kasey said. She'd been remarkably good since they'd hit the desert. No radio, no more books on tape, nothing to see except scrub, and sand, and distant mountains, nothing to do except bounce that Barbie for miles and miles and miles.

"I'm hot too, baby," Moira said, "but we're almost there."

At least she hoped they were. The little green road signs that had become her salvation—the ones listed how many miles she still had to travel to the end of each long day—told her that she wasn't far from Hawthorne.

But she saw no evidence of it. Except more signs, signs that didn't encourage her, most of them from the Adopt-A-Highway Program. The last section of road had been adopted by a bail-bonds company.

Good God, Gary, she'd thought when she saw it, *what the hell have you gotten us into?*

Only he hadn't gotten them into anything. He didn't even know they were coming. He would be surprised.

Guys like Gary always were.

— 2 —

Gary Storvick sat at his brand-new kitchen table, an ice-cold beer in his right hand. He'd set the air conditioner on frosty—Jenny and her global warming crap be damned—and sweat still ran down his back. He was as wet as if he'd taken a four-mile run at midday.

He hated it here, and he didn't look to leave any time soon.

The kitchen windows overlooking the dustbin that his wife called a yard actually tinted dark in the blazing Nevada sunlight. Whoever thought of building a town in the middle of a goddamn desert?

And who in their right mind thought of living here?

He pulled the bottle of beer closer, and stared at the cell phone he'd laid on the woven placemats Jenny had purchased in a fit of house beautifying. This place needed beautifying. A 1950s ranch, expanded in the 1970s, with a "modern" kitchen added in the 1990s.

He felt stifled here, like someone had taken the house he'd grown up in, added a few layers of paint, then sucked all the humidity out of it. He'd been raised in Wisconsin, thought he knew weather extremes, until he hit this place with its 120-degree summers and its fucking frosty winters.

The guys said he needed to get used to it. Just like fucking I-raq, they'd say. Like it mattered. The war had migrated to Afghanistan, which was nothing like Nevada except that it was empty and filled with mountains and land no one gave a rat's ass about.

He doubted he'd go to Afghanistan. They had sent him to Fallujah, then brought him home, then sent him to Baghdad, and brought him home, and in the debrief, they decided he was toxic, which really meant he knew too much about too many things and so they sent him here, where they could watch him and he was realistic enough to know that they'd sent him here because he still had something of value, when they could've just as easily sent him back over there and found him his own personal roadside bomb.

One disposable cell phone, sitting right in front of him, not ringing.

His regular cell phone, a two-year-old Nokia with a cheapo family plan, was clipped to the waistband of his jeans. He had a contract he couldn't get out of, something that seemed like a bargain at the time, but now looked so goddamn expensive he felt like someone had deliberately screwed him, even though he had made the choice himself.

Fucking phone still wasn't ringing. He glared at it. He'd expected the call early. He figured if they called early, he'd give them a good deal, because they had initiative.

You had to admire anyone with initiative.

But no one was calling. That was the thing. He'd expected them to call early. He'd taken out the paper the minute after Jenny had left. Address written clearly, storage locker number, and the combination, all waiting for his contact. Now the call was late. The cell was working; he'd checked, even though he wasn't supposed to. He'd called it at ten that morning using his Nokia, listening to the ring tones, becoming familiar with the way the screen lit up, the little notifications. He even figured out how to wipe his call out of the memory.

He was proud of himself for that.

It made for an interesting morning.

And now it was half past one, and he'd eaten lunch, and he was having a beer—just one—because it got goddamn hot in the freakin' desert, even with the air conditioner on frigid, and he couldn't take the fucking silence too fucking much longer.

He stood up, turned on the little kitchen TV he'd tucked between the stove and the sink just for Jenny so she could watch while she was cooking.

He used it more than she did, watching the news every morning while he ate the bacon and eggs he always had to cook himself.

Jenny didn't do breakfast.

Jenny didn't do much of anything.

It'd been a mistake to marry her, but how was he to know, deploying a second time, lonely as hell, wanting a little more than the series of one-night stands he'd survived on since Fallujah.

The irony was he had women friends. A couple of them, back in Wisconsin, back when they'd shipped him to Fort McCoy for one of those goddamn debriefs. Women he could actually talk to, women who would listen.

He didn't fuck them. He didn't touch them. The base counselor said he had commitment issues, but he didn't have that either.

He just thought—at the time anyway—he shouldn't mix business with friendship, and sex, in those days, was all business. In Wisconsin, he had women for talking and women for fucking. He never mixed the types. The talking women didn't even know that there were fucking women. The talking women thought he was lonely and harmless, and while he was lonely, he certainly wasn't harmless.

The fucking women had learned that. Some of them had learned that really, really well.

Just like a few of the talking women had learned a bit too much about his business, especially when he'd been drinking. He was happy to leave them behind.

At least at first.

Then he learned that there were always fucking women, but talking women were hard to find.

Until Jenny. Jenny, who was pretty and smart and all the things a guy could want in a wife. Jenny, who seemed like a good idea at the time.

She'd left the kitchen TV on Fox News. Some blowhard was yakking about the war, about troops and withdrawals and replacements and battlefield decisions, and from the look of the blowhard he'd never seen a battlefield outside of a frickin' war movie.

That was the problem with TV—didn't matter, Fox News, CNN, CBfuckinS—it was filled with blowhards who didn't know a goddamn thing about anything important.

Gary flicked the remote to ESPN, also filled with blowhards, but at least they knew what they talked about wasn't important. He turned the sound on low, so he could hear the phone ring.

If no one called before Jenny got home, he'd have to set the phone on vibrate and stuff it into his pockets. Maybe he should call her, tell her he was having some guys over to watch a game (was there a game?) and ask her (nicely, because she only responded to nice) to stay the fuck away tonight.

Or maybe he should wait another hour. She wasn't due home until five, wouldn't get here until five-fifteen earliest, even though it only took ten minutes to drive through all of Hawthorne. She'd stop at the store, chatter her way down the aisles, bring home some precooked crap for dinner.

He'd pretend to enjoy it, like he always did.

Unless he had a reason to get the hell out of here.

Unless he had a reason to fucking disappear.

He stared at the phone.

Ring, you son of a bitch, he thought. *Just fucking ring.*

— 3 —

The sunlight wasn't reflecting off the highway. It was reflecting off water, a huge large unbelievable lake of it, out in the middle of the longest stretch of desert she'd ever seen in her life. The signs—her only form of adult communication since that trucker in Salt Lake—gave her its name (Walker Lake) and the names of its beaches, but no clue as to whether the thing was natural or manmade.

The mountains had moved in closer. They butted up against the highway, inspiring those falling rock signs. The road ran between the cliffs and the lake—a ribbon of safety in the middle of a vast emptiness.

Ahead, her tired eyes could make out buildings—except that they shimmered like the heat mirages in 1930s movies. To her left, at the southern tip of that lake, rows and rows of buildings that seemed uniform, and directly behind the mountains, flat land again that appeared to have a few trees.

The wind tunneled through here, and created little waves on the surface of the lake itself. More ominous signs appeared—giving specific instructions to vehicles carrying ammunition.

Moira glanced at Kasey again. She couldn't read yet, and even if she could, she probably wouldn't know what ammunition was.

Moira didn't like it. She didn't like any of it.

Perhaps, when she had researched Gary, she should have researched Hawthorne, Nevada, as well.

She made it off the treacherous hillside and followed the road into that valley. Just as she entered town, another sign warned her that any vehicle *not* carrying ammunition stay away from the road that veered to her left.

She assumed that meant vehicles not designated to carry ammunition, not the handful of trucks she'd seen with full gun racks. As far as she knew, everyone out here carried a little ammunition, if for nothing else than their own personal firearm.

Moira glanced down the little road that veered to the left, and didn't see anything special. Although as she watched it fade into the distance, she realized it probably snaked its way to that group of uniform buildings she'd initially seen from the highway, the one later signs marked as the Hawthorne Army Depot and Ammunition Dump.

But, she reminded herself, she had lived near Fort McCoy in central Wisconsin, and the signs there were equally ominous—*No Cell Phones and Pagers Beyond This Point* (that had been relatively new, and quite curious; she'd never understood what they were afraid of); *Unauthorized Vehicles Subject to Military* (military what? she always wondered); *No Civilians Beyond This Point* (were they not allowed? Or were there none? She had no idea on that either).

She squared her shoulders and kept driving, trying to pretend that Hawthorne wasn't as awful as it seemed. On this end of town, a few roadside motels scattered amongst the sagebrush. They looked like no one had upgraded them for fifty years.

Normally Kasey would have seen a motel and asked if they could stop, but she remained silent. She wasn't asleep—Moira could hear the rustle of fabric as the doll bounced on her imaginary springs—but Kasey obviously didn't want to stay at any of those desolate places either.

"Gotta pee, honey?" Moira asked.

"Mmm-hmmm."

The problem was there wasn't many places Moira felt comfortable stopping at. The ubiquitous McDonald's—her friend in all the vast open spaces—had vanished in these small Nevada communities, and some of the truck stops weren't the kind of place you took a small child.

Still, she stopped at one just inside the Hawthorne city line—a small one that looked like a glorified gas station with showers—and after she and Kasey had completed their business, she asked the bored young clerk where the best food in town was, figuring in this obsolete place "best" meant "edible."

"The casino. But you gotta go in the right door. She—" the clerk nodded at Kasey, who was staring at the Milky Way bars beneath the cash register "—can't come within some weird feet of the slot machines."

It sounded like trouble.

But ever since Moira had turned down Highway 95, everything sounded like trouble. She'd been impatient to get here, and now that she was here, she wasn't sure if her plan—the one that had carried her all the way from Tomah six states away—had been such a good idea after all.

Kasey reached for the candy bar, making her decision.

Moira let Kasey put the candy bar on the counter, paid the two dollars (two dollars! For something that used to cost less than fifty cents!) and led Kasey back into the sunshine.

Moira's stomach growled, too, but she could wait. She didn't want to see the casino, not if Gary was home. And if he wasn't, she might visit one of those roadside motels, stay for at least one night, until she was able to find him.

While she had talked to the clerk, she'd studied a map of Hawthorne taped to the counter. There wasn't much to the city. Roads that trailed off into the desert, the highway threading through the middle, and half a dozen areas forbidden to all but military personnel.

But this wasn't like any base town she'd ever been to. Usually they were lively, filled with Walmarts and low-end grocery stores and a mall where everyone spent Saturday night. Bars stretched through the center of town, along with video stores and movie theaters, and support housing, not just for the overfill on the base, but for the civilian staff itself.

Here, the dusty wind blew like it could scrub the town clean. Except for a golf course not too far from that ominous sign, nothing recreational appeared. The truck stop offered a few videos, and large billboards promised gambling at the casino—the only one for a hundred miles, something that didn't sound promising either.

As she crested a hill into the town proper, she wondered how anyone could live here—and what they did to keep themselves sane.

She had looked up Gary's address on Google Earth before she left Wisconsin. She'd seen the satellite image of the little ranch houses that looked so uniform, so nice, from above.

The satellite image hadn't told her how godforsaken this town was.

At least Google Earth, along with a mapping program, had given her exact directions to the house Gary had actually purchased. That was what surprised her the most. Not that he had married, not that he was working on the side, but that he had actually bought a house.

What had he been thinking?

Knowing Gary, not much.

Gary wasn't a planner, like she was.

Only a handful of streets went toward the west. They led to actual neighborhoods, places where people lived.

They had looked so blessedly normal on Google Earth. Now that she was here, they looked desperate, like people were trying to make the best of a bad situation.

At least the yards were landscaped. That meant there was water here, and it wasn't rationed like Las Vegas. She liked the Midwest with its 10,000 lakes and its humidity. Water, water everywhere. Water, which enabled anyone to survive on her own for days if she had to, even if she had no food.

"What's that?" Kasey asked.

Moira turned slightly. "What, hon?"

"That pointy thing."

Moira had already slowed the van to a near-crawl so that she could look at street signs. But she'd been looking up, not down, getting a sense of well-tended (albeit old) ranch houses, beloved lawns, and large vehicles that seemed out of place with the 1950s elegance of the place.

She had to focus on the nearest lawn to see the "pointy thing."

And then she had to stifle a gasp.

It was a bombshell, probably as tall as Kasey, placed in the center of the landscaping along with several other shells to create a makeshift fence.

The yard next to it had a variation—bombshells and mortars—round and perfect, the size of a boulder—making her stomach twist.

Moira's hands slid on the old steering wheel, covered with sweat for the first time in days.

She had to keep going. She needed the money. She'd let the last run out too long ago. It wasn't that she liked the work. She was just good at it—good at all of it. She used to think it was because of her moon-shaped face, her diminutive frame, and her blond hair. People let her get away with stuff.

Then she realized that she wasn't just getting away with stuff. She was actively doing a job, a job most people couldn't—or wouldn't—do.

"What is it?" Kasey asked again, with a touch of impatience.

Moira had forgotten that a question was on the table. She gave the old-fashioned adult answer, the one that covered everything: "I'm not sure, honey. But it looks dangerous. Better stay away from it."

Gary lived at the end of one of those quiet streets. His yard had flowers—flowers she didn't recognize that seemed somehow exotic. The bombshells that created his fence had rust on the edges—something that shouldn't have been reassuring and somehow was. They predated his arrival here. Whomever he'd bought the house from had placed the shells in the yard and Gary, with his native caution, hadn't yet found a safe way to remove them.

A Jeep Wrangler was parked in the tiny driveway, Nevada plates half obscured by dirt. Moira pulled in behind it—she didn't want to park along the street next to those bomb tailings—and shut off the engine.

She rested her head on the steering wheel for one brief moment. God, she was tired. She hated being this tired. And sticky. Her arms ached from fighting that steering wheel in the wind.

Heat had already started to gather in the van. She couldn't sit here long, and Kasey couldn't sit here at all.

Moira sat up. "You do what I say for the next few minutes, okay, Kase?"

"Yes'm," Kasey said.

God, she was a good kid. That had been the surprise of the trip, what a good little traveler Kasey was. Moira hadn't expected it. She had expected Kasey to be a big problem.

Moira pulled the strap of her purse over her head, so that the strap would rest on one shoulder and the purse on the opposite hip. The purse weighed half a ton.

She opened the door, slid out into the heat, felt the sweat wick off her in a matter of seconds. She pulled open the back door, got Kasey out of the booster seat, and helped her onto the driveway.

Then Kasey extended a hand. "Who lives here?"

"A guy I used to know." Moira took Kasey's hand, careful to keep the giant purse on the other side.

"Do I know him?" Kasey asked.

"Probably not," Moira said.

They walked around the Jeep Wrangler, past some decorative brick paving stones that looked new, and up two steps to the tiny bit of concrete that 1950s ranch house designers would've called the front porch.

Then Moira pressed the doorbell. Faintly, she heard an old fashioned ding-dong.

Kasey looked up, then put one finger to her lips. In spite of herself, Moira smiled. Kasey remembered. No talking to strangers. Perfect.

Maybe this would work after all.

— 4 —

Gary looked at the phone when the doorbell rang. He expected to see the small screen light up, the phone vibrating its way across the top of the table. But the phone hadn't moved, and it took a moment for that to register.

Doorbell. Not some weird ring tone. Doorbell.

Which sounded again.

"Shit," he muttered. "Shitshitshitshit."

He didn't know what to do with the fucking phone. Finally he put it in the front pocket of his jeans. He pushed the chair back, took one more sip of beer—lukewarm now—and walked into the living room.

He'd make them go away, whoever the hell they were. The only people who rang the bell were the delivery people, the ones who helped Jenny with her home beautifying by bringing all the packages of crap she ordered off the Internet.

Just what he needed right now. Some eager, lost UPS guy who wanted to talk after being on the lonely roads between Hawthorne and Carson City, proud of himself for actually finding this godforsaken place.

Gary was going to grab the package and slam the door, no chatting, no directions, no discussion of the fucking weather, which was always the same, by the way, crappy as hell, hot, dry, and windier than anything anyone in Chicago had ever fucking imagined.

He pulled open the door, and paused, stunned.

He'd expected some reedy guy in a brown uniform, the panel truck idling on the street. Instead, a blond woman with a sunburned face stared at him. She wore a thin gauze shirt over some kind of spandex bra-like thing, and a tight pair of cut-offs. Her sandals had heels, which meant she wasn't from this part of Nevada. Vegas maybe, where shoes like that were practical. Not here.

"Gary?" she asked in a husky voice. "Can we come in?"

He blinked, saw the source of the "we"—there was a kid, a little girl, blonder (if that was possible) than the woman herself, and not sunburned, biting her lower lip and clutching a Barbie.

He'd never seen the kid before.

The woman, though. The woman—he knew her, but from somewhere else. God, he hated it when people were out of context. It took him forever to figure out who or what they were, where he knew them from.

Maybe he'd slept with her. Maybe the kid was his.

That would be a fucking goddamn nightmare come to life.

"Don't you remember me?" the woman asked, her tone plaintive. "Moira Clarkson. You know, we used to be neighbors—"

"In Tomah," he said with relief. "Shit—sorry."

He looked at the kid. He never was around kids, didn't know how to talk in front of them except not to swear.

Even though he wanted to. No way was this his kid. That was in his one-night stand days, back when the base shrink said he couldn't commit, back when he had more female friends than anyone else he knew.

"I would've called, but I can't afford a phone." She swept a hand at the driveway. He followed the movement, saw something—a van?—parked behind the Jeep. "Everything we've got's in there."

The little girl was weirdly quiet. He didn't remember Moira Clarkson having a kid. But what was that? Five, six years ago? Hell, she must've been pregnant when he knew her. Had the kid just after he deployed.

"I'm married," he blurted.

"I'm sorry," she said. "This won't take long. We just needed a place to stop. I hope that's okay?"

No, it's not okay. My wife'll kill me. The phone's gonna ring. You gotta get out before it does. I can't have anyone here right now.

The problem wasn't that he didn't have an excuse, but that he had too many. He hadn't planned for this. He didn't know how to handle this one.

Moira put her hand on the little girl's shoulder.

"I gotta pee," the little girl said calmly.

Did little kids say that calmly? Didn't they usually dance from foot to foot, get a panicked look, repeat themselves more than once, each time with increasing urgency?

Instead, this kid just looked at him, like she expected him to let her in.

"Sorry," Moira said. "Can we...?"

He sighed. "Make it quick."

They ducked inside. He pointed down the hall, but they were already heading that way. Maybe it was more of an emergency than he thought. Maybe the kid was just polite. Lots of Midwestern kids were, brought up with good values, some discipline. He'd seen the discipline here, too, but it was usually enforced with a fist, and Moira didn't seem the fisty type.

She wasn't tough at all. That's what he remembered about her. One of those perennial victims who always had some kind of boyfriend trouble.

He remembered her now. They'd spend hot summer evenings in back of the apartment complex at one of the picnic tables the manager put out every spring, drinking beer and shooting the shit. Mostly Gary listened. He liked practicing listening, figured it was good for business. Most people liked listeners. Listeners made people feel important.

So he listened and asked questions and became the guy women would touch (just a little drunkenly) and say, *You're a good friend, Gary. Really. Nice. Why'ren't most guys nice like you?*

Moira. She got him to talk, too. Just enough. She was one of those victimy women who made him feel important. Bragging to her was good. Bragging to her made him feel that talking women could be as good as fucking women.

He'd been wrong about that, though.

He glanced outside, saw no cars in the driveways. The street was mostly empty at this time of day anyway. Third shifters were asleep, everyone else was working. He'd heard that a lot of people used to have one spouse at home, but who could afford it now? Most folk in this neighborhood worked at the casino or the base, stashing money away.

The government don't take care of vets' families no more, his neighbor said one night. *Something bad happens, we gotta take care of our own.*

Which was what Gary was trying to do.

He shut the door.

No cars meant no one saw her van, which was good, because Jenny would ask questions. And this was the day he didn't want to answer questions. He was good at lying to most people, but Jenny expected the lies and grilled him like a drill sergeant. He'd choke, just like he did when Moira showed up, and then Jenny'd want to know what the hell was going on, and he wouldn't be able to figure out which lie to tell or if he should lie at all.

He wandered through the living room, with the leather sofa that cost one month's salary, and the flat-screen TV that Jenny couldn't live without, and peered into the kitchen, staring at the table.

He couldn't take the phone out now. He didn't dare. Moira might remember it.

He peered down the hall. The bathroom door was closed. How long did it take one little kid to pee?

And how the hell had they found him here? Why would Moira, of all people, come looking for him?

He went back into the living room and peered out the picture window, getting a good view of the van.

The thing looked worse for wear. That mattress on the top looked none too stable, and there were boxes in the back.

Fuck. She was running. Probably from one of the bad boyfriends or an ex-husband. Probably the kid's father.

Women like that, they looked for a friend, one most people wouldn't think of.

And dammit all to hell, that would be how he fit in.

He couldn't put her up, that's what he'd say, and that would be true—imagine how Jenny'd react to that—but he could give her some cash, maybe enough to get her to California or wherever the hell she was going.

Because she sure as shit wasn't staying here.

She had to know that. What had she said? *This isn't going to take long.*

Maybe she just meant the peeing. Or maybe she'd just said that to get into the house.

God, what a mess. And the phone wasn't ringing. He moved away from the window, and went to his emergency stash—built into the armrest of the unbelievably expensive couch. *A couch and a safe!* Jenny had said when she bought it like it was a fucking twofer kinda deal instead of a weird combination designed to jack up the price.

He pulled out four hundreds, hoping that would be enough, even though gas for that van had to be fifty bucks a pop easy. So he pulled out one more hundred, and stashed all the bills in the other front pocket of his jeans.

Then he shut the armrest, and started pacing again, wondering what was taking so long in the goddamn bathroom, wondering what he'd have to do to get them out of there, to get them out of here, to get them the hell out of his life.

— 5 —

Kasey perched on the folded-down toilet seat, sneakers dangling, fingers playing with the earbuds, trying to adjust them to her tiny ears. Moira had splurged on child-sized earbuds, knowing she'd need them. Then she filled the ancient iPod she'd bought on eBay with all kinds of weird kids' music, which Kasey loved.

The iPod was a special treat, because Moira didn't like Kasey to be lost in her own world. Too dangerous most of the time. Even kids—especially kids—had to pay attention to where they were and what was happening around them.

Except right now.

Although it was hard not to pay attention to this bathroom. It was one of those bathrooms that assaulted the senses, a bathroom afraid of its own function. Plush throw rugs and matching toilet lid covers which, if nothing else, had the benefit of softness. A matching cozy for the Kleenex, of all things, and a cover over the toilet paper.

The entire room smelled like Glade. Scented soaps sat in a shell tray, and the real soap dispensed out of a little sculpture hanging on the wall. Tiny decorative towels hung on the rack. The real towels were tucked inside the shower, as if someone were ashamed of them.

Men like Gary didn't have bathrooms like this. Men like Gary had bathrooms with hard water lines on the toilet, a towel bunched on the

19

floor instead of a rug; bathrooms that smelled of toothpaste and Old Spice and pee.

Men like Gary only had bathrooms like this when they had wives with Definite Ideas, wives who believed a house doubled as a home and a showplace.

Wives who would worry if they knew their husband entertained a strange woman in the middle of the afternoon.

Moira had to hurry.

She ran her hand over Kasey's thin hair. Kasey gave her a wan smile, then looked away just like she was told. She bobbed her head to the music that (thankfully) Moira couldn't hear.

Moira wished the bathroom was less 1950s, more modern. She needed one closet area, a place for a moment of privacy. She wasn't going to get it.

So she turned slightly, facing the door, but with her back to the mirror and to Kasey. Moira reached inside her bag, found the .38, and checked to make sure it was loaded (it was). Then she checked the silencer, which she left attached to the barrel. Silencers were best in neighborhoods, particularly neighborhoods with the houses this close together.

No one would mistake a gunshot for a car backfiring here. Everyone would know exactly what they heard. But the silencer—while not quite the lovely little *thwap* that it had on television—would muffle things enough that not even Kasey, with her iPod on relatively low, would hear anything.

Moira's heart pounded. She made herself take a deep breath.

She kept her right hand on the gun, and let herself out of the bathroom.

The hall was dark, claustrophobic. Pictures hung on each wall, one wedding picture, then family portraits, mostly of the wife, whoever the hell she was.

Gary peered into the hall. She could sense his nervousness from here. He didn't want her in the house. He didn't know what she wanted, and he clearly worried about what his wife would think.

"It'll take her just another minute," Moira said with a smile.

"She okay?" He sounded concerned, but not concerned for a little girl. Concerned for himself, a panicked kind of concern, as in *hurry the hell up and get out of here.*

"Yeah. She has a nervous bladder. Sometimes she just needs privacy."

He nodded as if he understood, which he probably didn't, not that it mattered. What mattered was getting him out of the living room and into the back of the house.

"How'd you find us?" he asked. *Us*, not *me.*

"Internet," she said. "You can find anything on the Internet."

He nodded, then peered around her at the bathroom.

"She can probably hear us," Moira said. "Is there somewhere a little more private?"

He gave her a desperate look. "My wife'll be here soon—"

"I understand," Moira said.

"I don't know why you were looking for me…." And then the desperate look again. Not so much panic over their presence as over Kasey's. He probably wondered if Moira was going to slap him with a paternity suit.

Not that it was possible. They both knew nothing had happened. She had made sure of that. But that didn't stop some men from worrying. Some men's lives got ruined just by the accusation.

Probably Gary's would too.

Not that it mattered.

"Let's go into the kitchen," she said softly.

His gaze met hers. "If it's money—"

"The kitchen," she said.

He sighed, and walked through the living room, past the expensive television and the showy couch, past the glass-topped coffee table and the shelves covered with carefully laid out knickknacks, into a kitchen that had been remodeled at least once in this house's history.

Another television ran *Sports Center*. A half-full beer bottle sat next to a piece of paper on a woven placemat. Fake fruit in a cut-glass bowl had been moved to one side of the table.

The kitchen, at least, looked used.

"Moira," he said. "I don't know why you're here or what you want from me. I'm not in the position to help you."

"I know," she said.

She pulled out the gun, the movement swift and clean. One shot, right at his chest—take the wider shot first, she always said—knocking him back against the counter. His hand clutched at the counter's edge, and he looked at her in utter confusion.

He slid down to the floor and she shot him again, in the chest again. His eyes glazed and he slumped to one side.

He wasn't dead. Not yet. It would take him a minute or two to bleed out.

She knew better than to touch him. He'd had a lot of field training. If he could move, he would, and he would grab her. She wasn't going to get close enough for that.

Blood pooled. His face grew waxen.

Finally the blood stopped pumping.

He might not be dead yet, but by the time she gathered up Kasey, he would be.

Moira checked the floor. No blood had seeped this far.

Then she looked at her clothes. No spatter—at least, no obvious spatter.

She reloaded the gun, then stuffed it inside her purse. She loved revolvers. No casings. A good old-fashioned gun for a good old-fashioned job.

She paused and stared at the beer. God, it looked good. She grabbed the piece of paper and used it to pick up the beer so that she didn't leave fingerprints. She almost took one sip, then thought the better of it, and set the beer down.

She slipped out of the kitchen, and headed down the hall to the bathroom.

Moira opened the bathroom door.

Kasey was rocking and bouncing the Barbie in time to her music.

Moira ran a hand over her blond head. "You ready to go, baby doll? she asked.

Kasey nodded, but made no move to remove the earbuds. For once, Moira didn't make her.

Instead, she took Kasey's hand and led her out of the bathroom. They walked through the showy living room, Moira's body blocking any view of the kitchen, and out the front door as if their visit had ended.

"Say bye-bye, baby doll," Moira said.

Kasey turned, smiled, waved with her free, non-Barbie hand.

"Bye!" she said in her loudest voice.

God, the kid was good.

They went to the van. Moira stashed her purse under the dash, then buckled Kasey into the booster seat in the back.

"How about some lunch?" Moira asked as she climbed into the front seat.

"Mickey D's!" Kasey said.

"Not today, baby," Moira said. "I'm thinking someplace different."

Someplace more visible.

Someplace memorable.

"You ever been to a casino?" Moira asked, and started to drive, not waiting for an answer.

— 6 —

Davis watched the broken-down van pull out of the driveway, moving precariously, the mattress on the top secured with only two bungee cords. He stood near the picture window, leaning back just a little so that no one could see him from across the street.

Not that people would notice him. No one noticed middle-aged men, particularly if they weren't threatening. He wore baggy clothes, pouched out to make him look heavier than he was, although he probably didn't have to do that.

There were a lot of athletic forty-something guys in Hawthorne, especially guys with short hair and good posture. The military didn't like its members going to fat.

But he kept his fitness hidden, just like he kept his face down when he walked through the neighborhood.

A man couldn't be too careful.

So far as he could tell, no one had noticed him so far. He and his team had remained invisible to the entire neighborhood, not that there was much of one. Most people on this block had either deployed or moved away. The few who were left worked third shift, and cared only about sleep when they got home.

No one looked inside the thin curtains covering the picture window. If they had, they would have guess that the owners cared a lot about gadgetry.

The living room was furnished with a blue couch and chair bought new from Hawthorne's only furniture store, a coffee table from Goodwill that was now covered with coffee cups and old newspapers, and a big-screen television set tilted away from the window because it mostly showed videos of the neighborhood itself.

A camera sat on one side of the picture window and on the other, an expensive computer setup that probably cost more than the house itself. You had to lean against the picture window to see the computer.

But it wasn't hard to see out from the computer station. Davis actually caught the van out of the corner of his eye even before it showed up in the cameras he'd placed throughout the neighborhood. The van bothered him, mostly because he hadn't seen a visitor at Gary Storvick's house since Davis had started watching it a month before.

Now a petite blonde with a kid and Wisconsin plates pulls up, goes inside, stays barely a half an hour, and leaves, looking discouraged. Only the little girl seemed cheerful, waving in that oblivious way little kids had.

Storvick hadn't even come to the door to see them out.

The van made its way up the street and turned toward the center of town. Davis already had the plates, not that they would do him a lot of good. He'd try to run them himself, but the programs he had access to weren't that great. He had a few friends he could ask, but he wasn't sure it was worth his time.

Storvick knew the woman, that was clear by the expression his face as he let them in. The kid had seemed like a surprise to him.

Storvick had been stationed in Wisconsin before his last deployment. He hadn't made a lot of waves there, although he had some complaints, mostly from women who thought he'd treated them too rough on dates. His records from the time seemed typical—lots of one-night stands, mostly from late-night bar hookups, a handful of friends he kept distant from each other.

Already he'd been working the money, making a few contacts, making some plans.

Not that it had been in his file. His official file was unexceptional—regular soldier who did what he was told and nothing more. A few things showing up on his tests—scores indicating anti-social personality in his MMPI, a few warning signs in his Myers-Briggs, things that had been unusual when he enlisted post-9/11, but weren't now. The all-volunteer Army had lowered its standards a few years ago to keep up with the recruitment numbers. Storvick would've fit into that new group.

The surprise was that he wasn't new. He'd been part of the regular Army long before real criminals were given a choice between jail and Iraq.

Which, in Davis's personal opinion, only made Storvick smarter than the average recruit. He'd known his tendencies, maybe thought the military would work them out of him, never expecting the lawlessness that was Iraq in the early years, was Afghanistan now.

Davis went back to his own computer. The camera he'd installed in Storvick's backyard showed sunlight glinting off the gas grill like it did every afternoon at this time, a lawn chair that had been overturned for days now thanks to last week's wind, and some anemic houseplants soaking up too much light on what passed for a deck.

The glare-resistant glass of the kitchen windows showed nothing. Even if there was something to see, Davis wouldn't be able to see it. Not at this time of day.

And he hadn't been able to get into the place to plant bugs or cameras. Someone always seemed to be home. The one time Davis tried to install bugs, Jenny the wife had showed up unexpectedly. He barely made it out the back door and through the fence before she brought some groceries into the kitchen.

None of the cameras he'd installed in the neighborhood showed anything. So he had no visuals.

He had no audio either. Storvick hadn't received a call on either of his cells—the cheap family cell or the expensive cell his partner had given him back in Wisconsin. Storvick had gotten a call two days ago on the expensive cell, setting up another call for 1 o'clock today, but that call hadn't come in, on this cell, the other cell, or the landline. Davis had managed to tap the landline, and he'd hacked into Storvick's cells so that any call that went to Storvick also came through this computer. He'd listened to a lot of inane crap, most of which he complained about.

Today, he'd've given anything for inane crap. Instead, silence.

Even Storvick's e-mail account was silent, except for the usual spam and forwards from friends still deployed. No computer activity either—no instant messages, no Tweets, no dinking around on Facebook.

Whatever the hell Storvick was doing in there, he was doing it quietly.

Which irritated Davis all the more.

The contact was supposed to be today. By phone. What was he waiting for?

Maybe he called it off when the blond showed up. She was clearly unplanned for. She almost looked like she was near tears when she left. The kid was what? Five? Six? Old enough to be Storvick's if something had gone wrong.

What Davis wouldn't have given to be a fly on that wall. Not just because of the contact—hell, the contact was the least interesting part of the day. He just wanted to know what had happened with the woman. Was she an old girlfriend? Did she threaten a paternity suit? Was she trying to scam money from her old friend?

Then he frowned.

Was she the contact? With a little girl?

It would be a smart move. No one would suspect her.

She could be driving off in that crummy van of hers with the address for fifteen million dollars in her back pocket—and no one would be the wiser.

He grabbed his cell phone, dialed.

"Think we might've missed the contact," he said without preamble.

"How the hell's that possible?" Dirksen asked, sounding tinny—not in his office then, but somewhere else. Horns, voices in the background. City street? Far from here, that was for damn sure.

"Blond woman and a kid showed up half an hour ago. There've been no calls, no Internet traffic. Just her. They left a little while ago."

"You didn't think to follow?"

"It's my job to monitor the house," Davis snapped. "You want that kind of operation, you give me more manpower."

"Get the plates?"

"Sure, but I don't have the capability to run them, not that it matters. She should be easy to find." He explained the cruddy van, the mattress, the Wisconsin plates. "There's only two ways out of this town—north on 95 and south on 95. I'll go south if you get Lyman to go north."

"Then who'll monitor the house?"

"Have one of your guys do it from there. The wife'll be home in an hour. No one'll call when she's there."

"I'm sending the kid," Dirksen said. "You wait till he gets there."

"And risk losing her?"

"You ever been south on 95?" Dirksen asked. "You can be an hour behind her, and you'll still see her. There's a lot of nothing out there."

Davis shuddered. When he came to Hawthorne a month ago, he'd come from the north. There was a whole lot of nothing up there. He wasn't thrilled about even more nothing.

Although it was better than being holed up in this house much longer, watching a guy who—if it weren't for his access to $15 million in misplaced hundreds—would seem no different from any other married grunt in this overheated hellhole.

"Find out who she is," Davis said. "Maybe I won't have to chase her. Maybe she's got nothing to do with this."

"Would you have called me if you believed that?"

Davis paused. He hated the way Dirksen could read him. "No."

"All right then. The kid'll be there in thirty. I'll see what I can find, but don't expect much. Sometimes contacts use vulnerables to get to the primary."

Davis hated it when Dirksen talked like that. "I know," he said.

Which was probably why the woman looked so lost, clutched the little girl's hand so hard.

Threaten someone's child and that someone'll do anything. Making her the vulnerable. Making her the tool of someone else.

Davis sighed. The afternoon had just gone from tense to strange.

And he had a hunch it would get a whole lot stranger before the day was out.

— 7 —

The restaurant inside the casino was an old-fashioned diner, the kind Moira hadn't seen since she was a kid. It even smelled old-fashioned—baked-in grease, cigarettes, and perfume. No one was smoking—she wasn't even sure people could still smoke in restaurants in Nevada—but the place was so old the stench of long-ago cigarettes still coated every single surface.

Five other people sat in the room. Four were truckers, judging by their conversation—thin men with greasy hair and cap lines, their caps hanging from a peg beside the booth. Old-fashioned men, who didn't wear hats inside, even though no one would probably ever notice.

A woman sat in the corner booth, a briefcase on the seat beside her. She wore a linen business suit, wrinkled from the heat, and nylons that had to be uncomfortable as hell. Her matching cream-colored heels knocked against each other under the table. She checked her BlackBerry, tapping in something while a half-eaten sandwich sat neglected on the tabletop.

She looked as out of place as Moira felt.

The waitress carried a tray of pastries to the truckers. She was a big-busted woman whose pile of red hair clashed with her gold-and-white uniform. She put the pastries down, flirted a minute with the truckers—who had to be regulars—and then set the tray down as she pivoted on one foot to walk to Moira's table.

Moira already had her coffee. Kasey's extra-special chocolate milk was half gone. The waitress, whose name—Jenny—was embroidered across those unavoidable breasts, gave Kasey a sincere smile.

"What can I getcha, hon?"

Kasey looked at Moira. "Happy Meal," she said, knowing she was pushing her luck.

"We don't got that, hon," the waitress said, undeterred. "But we got the best PB&J in Nevada. You want one?"

Kasey loved a good peanut butter and jelly sandwich. The next moment would be a toss-up between her mood and her favorite food.

"Can I have cake too?" she asked Moira. Kasey had already stopped in front of the rotating dessert display, which did have one of the best-looking selection of desserts Moira had seen in years.

"If you got room when you're done," Moira said.

Kasey grinned. "PB&J," she said to the waitress as if it were her idea.

The waitress wrote it down, then looked at Moira. "She's cute."

"Yeah," Moira said as if she heard that all the time. "Your burgers good?"

"Fried chicken's better," the waitress said.

"Okay," Moira said. "With fries."

She'd share them with Kasey, yet another treat. The girl'd been good—better than expected, in fact—so good that Moira would actually miss her.

The waitress headed off to the old-fashioned order window and actually put the piece of paper on a wheel, then spun it for the short-order cook. The way things used to be, before computers and touch screens and automatic portion control.

Moira glanced over her shoulder at the entrance to the restrooms. She'd checked it out as they came in. The setup was as old-fashioned as the restaurant itself. Two bathrooms, barely big enough for the required handicapped door, and a bank of pay phones between them.

She didn't remember the last time she'd seen a bank of pay phones. Usually, there was just one, with a ruined handset and no phonebook at all.

"I'm going over there," she said to Kasey, pointing. "You'll be able to see me the whole time."

Kasey nodded, but didn't look alarmed. Maybe after her last year, she didn't need to look alarmed. Maybe nothing could alarm her anymore.

Moira got up, looked longingly at the woman's BlackBerry, and then went to the counter. There she changed a five into quarters, not knowing how much she'd need.

Then she went to the pay phones, taking the one in the middle, which looked damn near new.

She punched in the number from memory, inserted the quarters, remembering when one quarter bought ten minutes and a dollar's worth was more time than any real phone call ever needed.

Analyn answered on the first ring. "What took so long?"

"Hello to you, too," Moira said.

"Where are you?" God, she sounded panicked. Moira hated it when they panicked.

"We're in Nevada. We'll be there tonight."

"Tonight? I thought you'd get here this morning."

"Had a side trip." Moira watched Kasey. She was bouncing the Barbie doll again. Moira wondered what the kid was thinking as that doll went up and down and up and down.

"Where are you then?"

"Having lunch in some diner. We've got about five hours of steady driving. Make sure you got a safe place to crash. She'll be exhausted."

"I'm sure she already is," Analyn said. "Driving all that way from Wisconsin. Flying would've been easier."

"Flying would've been impossible," Moira said, trying not to sound impatient. They'd been through this before. "They want twenty forms of ID now and they check it. We never woulda got outta the airport."

"Still, to make a little girl drive that far—"

"To make a little girl drive that far was the only way you'd get her," Moira said. "You better have the money when I see you."

"It's waiting," Analyn said.

"I need five K in cash," Moira said. "The other fifteen goes into the account I gave you."

"Cash? You didn't say anything about cash." Analyn sounded even more panicked.

"I just did," Moira said. "Five K. Cash."

"O-Okay."

"When I get there."

"Okay."

"I'm not going to pick up the cash. Got that?"

"Yes," Analyn said. She was beginning to sound calmer. Instructions usually did that for people. Instructions calmed them.

"You got the new phone number?"

"Yes," Analyn said, then rattled off some numbers.

Moira didn't write them down. She didn't have to. She never had to. Numbers stuck in her head like the choruses of bad songs.

"Now remember," she said, "ditch this phone."

"But…."

Moira had expected that. People didn't like to get rid of expensive things. "At least turn it off. Power off. No signal, not even for Internet. You got that. No power at all."

"I don't see why—"

"Trust me," Moira said. "I've done this a hundred times. When I get there, you give me the phone you're using now. Okay?"

"Okay."

"See you. Five hours, maybe six. You know where."

"Can't I call you?"

"I'll call you at the hotel if we're running late," Moira said, and hung up.

The truckers had talked through her entire conversation. The waitress was delivering the PB&J. Kasey looked happy, so maybe the waitress was right. Maybe it was the best PB&J in Nevada.

The fried chicken didn't look half bad either. Moira was hungrier than she expected.

The woman with the BlackBerry was gone, leaving a half-eaten salad, a five pressed against her plate, and a crumpled napkin. Back to the highway, where the restaurant at the casino would just be a bad memory.

Funny thing. Moira knew the woman had hated the place, but she didn't. She'd love to be a regular here, try all the pies, get to know if the fried chicken really was better than the burgers. She'd love to stop moving again.

It was time.

Or near time.

Not today. Not tomorrow. Maybe the next day.

When she was clear.

She was nearly done.

The key was to remember that the job wasn't over until every detail was complete.

— 8 —

Analyn's hands were shaking. She looked at the phone, searching for the off-switch. The more complicated these things got, the harder they were to power down.

She finally found the switch, pressed it, and waited for the electronics to hum to a close. Then she stashed the phone in her purse.

She looked around and made sure no one was watching her. A gondolier sang some terrible Italian love song. His voice echoed in the fake outdoors. The tourists in his gondola—honeymooners, most likely (real honeymooners, not the got-drunk-and-married-last-night types, but the ones who spent half their life savings on a ceremony that probably wouldn't last)—looked at him as if he were Sinatra come back to life.

They didn't seem to notice how fake it all was, the way that the canal smelled of chlorine. The way that the sunlight filtering through the fake Venetian sky couldn't mask that this was indoors.

She sat in a wire sweetheart chair, her purse resting on a round table. The snotty waiter had brought her an espresso about ten minutes before. He checked on her through the windows of the café, as if she were outside and he was inside.

She turned her back to him slightly, then pulled out the new phone and turned it on, making sure it worked. But there was no real way to test it. Moira be damned. Analyn was going to make sure the new phone at least rang.

She leaned back in her chair and slowly surveyed her surroundings. She tried not to look suspicious, but she probably was. Someone was watching her from one of those cameras, wondering what she was up to.

Or maybe they just assumed she was wasting time while her husband played cards or slots or whatever people did in these places. She had no idea. She had never been anywhere like this before.

The gondolier had dropped off the honeymooners and was waiting for more passengers. He had to stay near his gondola for his entire shift.

She felt a moment's fleeting compassion for him. Poor guy. She'd hate having a job like that, rowing (poling?) people through the clear water, making sure they had a good time, singing weird Italian love songs at the top of your lungs.

Not that she could sing. Even if she had a voice, she wouldn't be able to sing to people, and certainly not at the top of her lungs.

It was strangely quiet in here without his singing. The place felt like a damp morgue, just waiting for people to liven it up. There wasn't even Muzak overhead—probably because it would interfere with the singers.

She sighed. The waiter hovered near the window, but after she'd ordered the espresso she didn't want and then dismissed him twice, he knew better than to approach her unless she signaled, which she wasn't going to do.

The only other person in sight was a heavyset woman in an MGM Grand T-shirt and a pair of ill-advised shorts. The woman wandered in and out of the expensive shops as if she could get in trouble just by window-shopping inside them.

No one else in hearing range, and no one else who really seemed to care what Analyn was doing.

She pulled the shut-off phone out of her purse. Then she pressed the same button she'd used to turn it off. When that didn't work, she tried something else.

For a long moment, she thought she was cursed, that the phone would never come back on. Finally it powered up with a cheerful little tune, displaying a logo she would have changed if she was allowed to keep the phone longer.

Allowed to.

As if Moira controlled her life.

Although at the moment, Moira did.

Analyn punched in the new number, then hit "send." The other phone rang. She picked it up. The display showed the old number. She answered out of reflex, then hung up, and let out another sigh.

The new phone worked.

She powered down the old phone and put it in her purse. Then she deleted the number of the old phone from the new phone.

It was pristine, waiting for Moira to call.

Five hours, maybe six.

More than enough time to get the cash and get to the meet site.

More than enough time.

So why did she feel like she had to hurry?

Maybe because so much time had passed already.

Too much time. Time she and Kasey would never ever get back.

— 9 —

Davis paced. Living room to kitchen to hall to bedroom to hall to bedroom to hall to living room. The only room he didn't march in and out of was the bathroom, mostly because the place depressed him. It was as filthy as that coffee table. They hadn't cleaned it in three weeks, a mess of towels, garbage, and porcelain stains.

No one cleaned; waiting for someone else to do it, he supposed. Or maybe because they were so short-staffed they worked one man per shift, not always great during third shift, when the Storvicks slept and the neighborhood was even more quiet than usual.

He'd come in at 3 a.m. four nights ago to find Lyman watching a porn flick on the big-screen TV. For all he knew the man had his dick out until he heard the car door slam. He'd torn Lyman a new asshole, but privately didn't blame him.

Surveillance was tough, particularly alone, particularly when the surveyed were damn near normal in every way.

If he hadn't read the reports, if he hadn't heard Storvick talking, he would never have believed the man had access to fifteen million dollars.

Fifteen million dollars in hundreds. That kept Davis awake at nights, doing the math. That was 150,000 bills, bundled in 150 stacks, on a pallet somewhere, waiting to be dispersed.

Fifteen million dollars wasn't as hard to hide as it sounded. Someone had peeled it from a shipment heading to Iraq in 2003. Or several someones. He never heard all the details, wasn't sure if Gary Storvick was in command of all the details. Dirksen believed it, and verified it as best he could.

Dirksen, who had been in Iraq when 8.8 billion dollars in cash went missing. When a small-time arms dealer and contractor, later murdered, decided to confess to running a network of bribery in the U.S.-operated Green Zone in Baghdad. The man claimed that tens of thousands routinely went from officials and others in pizza boxes.

Pizza boxes. 8.8 billion, unaccounted for.

Early reports said 9 billion. Early reports weren't rounding up. They included other shipments, shipments that supposedly went to Iraq but got diverted at the docks and warehouses, siphoned off.

That money could be tracked just by weight, or so Dirksen had told him. Dirksen said some of the cash sat for seven years so that it wouldn't be so suspicious.

And somehow—Davis didn't know how—Storvick had learned where the cash was.

What Davis didn't get was why the idiot was selling the location instead of taking the cash for himself.

Maybe he'd already taken his cut. Maybe he was going to get something in exchange for the 15 million. Davis never did find out, and the brief phone messages and IMs didn't give him a clue.

Not that it was his business. He was making more than enough to compensate him for his time. He was a private contractor too. He ran the operation, such as it was, but he had to work with Dirksen's people—Lyman, and the kid. Dirksen was running the operation on the cheap, hiring Davis only and not Davis's guys. Davis's guys cost 10K per day, half of Davis, but they had expertise, expertise that Lyman and the kid couldn't learn in years of doing things Davis's way.

Not his concern. His concern had been getting the information, that was it. Listening to the conversation, figuring out where the meet was, maybe impersonating the buyer.

But over the last few weeks, he'd figured out he wasn't comfortable with the impersonation, since he didn't know exactly what—if anything—was being exchanged. He was just going to get to the address first, maybe even without informing Dirksen, and take his cut.

Unrecorded money could be a rumored fifteen million, maybe a million or so shy. Dirksen wouldn't know where the million went and Davis would just consider it a bonus for working with amateurs.

He hated amateurs.

He looked at his watch.

Thirty minutes since the van left. Twenty minutes. He could've caught up to her by now, maybe found out what she knew, maybe discovered if she was even a person he was interested in.

But no, he had to wait for the kid on Dirksen's orders. The kid who moved at his own pace, no matter how many fires Davis lit underneath him.

Kitchen door creaked open. Davis, in the living room, went to the sound.

The kid was setting a bag of groceries on the cluttered kitchen counter.

"What the fuck?" Davis said. "You were supposed to get here as fast as possible."

"We were out of stuff," the kid said. He was a scrawny twenty-five but looked sixteen. In a town full of military kids, he stood out, the obligatory slacker, T-shirts and jeans at half-mast.

Davis had complained about that, too. He didn't want someone visible. He wanted someone who disappeared.

Dirksen said a slacker kid didn't disappear, but he didn't get noticed either. Automatically dismissed as someone unimportant.

Because, Davis wanted to counter, the kid *was* unimportant.

"Look," the kid was saying, "if I'm supposed to work an extra shift, I need—"

"Fuck that," Davis said. "You might've lost our lead."

"What lead?" the kid said. "Dirksen said the contact didn't call."

"No, she might've shown up," Davis said. "I was supposed to follow her."

"Oh." The kid's voice sounded small. "Sorry, man. I didn't get the memo."

"Fucking amateur," Davis said. "You monitor house and cell and every-fucking-thing else. There've been no calls since she left, no computer activity either. So I think she's our contact. But just in case she isn't, you stay vigilant. Got that? It's your ass if we miss this."

The kid flushed, making the rest of his face the same color as the acne covering his chin.

Davis pointed at the living room. "Go!" he said.

The kid didn't have to be told twice. He left the groceries on the countertop and scrambled into the living room.

Davis rummaged in the grocery bag, found a box of energy bars, and snagged it. Then he headed out the kitchen door.

He hoped Dirksen was right. He hoped he'd catch the van somewhere south on 95. He hoped Lyman was bright enough to call if he saw the damn thing heading north.

Wild-goose chase. All because they hadn't thought of the possibility of a real-time meet.

The entire operation was marked with a lot of "hadn't thoughts." Should've charged more when he realized that he'd be the only experienced guy on the team.

Shoulda woulda coulda.

Too late now.

He headed down the block to his car, glad it had some speed hidden in its nondescript sedan's frame. Cop makeover, even though he wasn't a cop.

Cops got paid crap for doing the same things he did better than they ever could.

Cops wouldn't be able to touch the girl if they found her.

He could.

He could do anything he damn well pleased.

— 10 —

No one came for her. No one asked her questions. That was the beauty of being a slight woman who traveled with a kid, a kid who waved, smiled, and said, "Bye!" on command.

Moira glanced over her shoulder into the backseat. Barbie had stopped bouncing before the van even hit Highway 95. Kasey had fallen asleep, head lolling. Once Moira had asked a cop if it was safe to strap a sleeping child prone on the backseat using two seatbelts.

Probably, the cop said. *But someone'll complain if they look in your window, and if it's another cop, expect a fine. Zero tolerance for driving without a car seat. Too many of us have come up on accidents with dead kids who'd still be alive if it weren't for someone being too lazy to use a car seat.*

Not that she was too lazy. She followed the rules of driving—it kept the cops off her back at inconvenient times—but she remembered traveling as a kid, sprawling all over the back seat, sitting on the wheel well in a station wagon, crowding onto the floor with her shoulder blades pressed into the seat in front of her.

She had liked the freedom of travel, the fantasy she had of opening the door and rolling out, like the guys did on cop shows, then running, running, running, until she couldn't run any more.

Then she'd be in a new place with a new family and she could start all over again.

But even back then cars had child locks, so the one time she tried it hadn't worked. And then later she learned that Child Protective Services or whatever the hell it was called in whatever the hell state she found herself in would take a stray child and hold her for forty-eight hours, hoping someone would claim her, and if no one did, she would be "in the system," which seemed to be the same system everywhere, even if the name of the damn agency was different.

She'd been in the system five times all told. Each time, her mother had come for her, promising to be clean, promising that this new husband would be better. But the promises didn't last. The new husband would always be the same as the old—sometimes Moira wondered if it was just the old husband in a new husband suit, this one tall and thin, that one short and fat—and then the drinking would start, later the drugs. The drugs were the worst because they could make her mom into someone else. Drunk mom was mean. Drugged mom was gone or flaky or dumb.

Moira couldn't stand *dumb*. She'd take *mean* over *dumb* any day, and often did.

The City of Hawthorne hadn't gone on for very long. A few more neighborhoods, some gas stations, the McDonald's. A couple of other franchises whizzed past—was that a Tasty Freeze? Were there still Tasty Freezes in the world?—and then, down a crest, and suddenly she was in a vast expanse of reddish-brown desert that seemed to continue forever into the distance.

She hated this highway, had always hated this highway, even though she could go 120 miles per hour on it—if the stupid van had been able to go that fast. She hated this highway for the heat and the desolation and the way it made her feel vulnerable. If the van broke down, she'd burn up, and then what would happen to Kasey, Kasey whom she'd slathered with sun block against all her protests while standing in the parking lot of the casino for all the world to see.

If anyone had wanted to catch her that was the place, and she had half expected it. *Ma'am*, the cop would say, *can we talk for a moment?*—all polite because Kasey was there. The cop's partner would keep Kasey busy, maybe even make her laugh, while the cop himself would hitch up his britches and say, *Someone saw your van outside Gary Storvick's place. He's been shot. Did you have reason to kill him, Miss—?*

No, she'd say, *no, of course not,* and she'd sound innocent because innocent was something she practiced, innocent was as much a part of her job as the silencer and the quick maneuvers and the planned escape route. Innocence—or the appearance of it—was her guarantee.

But no one approached her at the casino. A cop car pulled out in front of her near the McDonald's, then turned on his lights and did a sweeping U-turn, but he didn't come after her.

Twenty-five times, she'd expected someone to come after her, and twenty-five times, no one had. The interrogations, so far, had all been in her head.

Sometimes she wondered if she'd even believe it if a cop spoke to her about one of the shootings. The only time, the one and only time, a cop had come up to her after a shooting, he'd helped her with the booster seat, and she'd asked her question, and he'd given her that oh-so-sincere answer which she pondered as she drove away, wondering if he had known after all and if he had just decided to let her get away because she was so pretty, the way cops let speeders get out of tickets—that promise of sex, with the sex never given. Kinda like her mother's promise of a clean life with a reputable man. The kind of promise that never ever came true.

The road vanished into the distance. The mountains etched against the sky didn't frame the area like mountains usually did. Instead, they seemed vaguely menacing, as if she even approached them wrong, she would die.

She wished she hadn't taken this route. She should've gone back, up through Carson City, and into California.

But that would've taken her miles out of the way, and that road was just as desolate, only a different kind of desolate.

This road would get her to Vegas quicker. Besides, there was other traffic here, truckers taking goods from Hawthorne to Tonopah to Beatty. Goods came to Vegas through Interstate 15. Vegas was the real world, with neon and malls and too much traffic. Highway 95 from Hawthorne to Beatty, past the Nevada Test Site and other ignominious sites, well, that wasn't the real world, that was a nightmare world where anything could go wrong.

Anything at all.

She sighed. She should have expected the mood. The mood always came on her after a successful mission. She got reminiscing and then she felt sad and then she got scared, and she hated scared.

Scared made her want to do things, made her want to try things she shouldn't try, made her do the unthinkable.

So she looked over her shoulder again at Kasey.

The job wasn't done until she got to Vegas. She had to remember that. Vegas was her final destination, not Hawthorne.

And once she finished the job, she could be scared or angry or crazy. She could do the unthinkable.

After Vegas.

Not before.

— 11 —

Davis drove like a crazy man through town. Blew two stoplights, narrowly avoided a giant truck with jacked-up over-inflated wheels and five different color *Support Our Troops* bumper stickers. The bumper stickers caught his eye instead of the driver, whom he assumed was young, male, and scared, certain he would be deployed and not sure how well he'd do in This Man's Army.

Well, Davis was there to tell him that it didn't matter how well you'd do. You'd survive or you wouldn't. You'd succeed or you wouldn't. You'd die or you wouldn't.

Then you'd be done and all those skills you learned, everything you'd been taught, all you could really excel at, well, no one needed those skills on the home front, not except the cops and they wouldn't want you if you were too military or too bright, if you closed too many cases by cutting too many corners. The cops wouldn't like you and private security was a racket.

Better to go off on your own, except when you worked for a cheap-ass idiot like Dirksen, Dirksen who wanted to get 15 million dollars without working for it, and without sharing it with his own private troops.

Traffic was always thin in Hawthorne except during shift change at the base, and even then what went through the town wasn't traffic so much as a few more cars. He was south of the base, anyway, so it didn't matter, just a few joy riders and military wives picking up groceries. Not even a cop usually, because Hawthorne didn't really need cops, not with so many tight-assed military hotshots who took their oath way too seriously.

With the number of guns in this town, Lyman said one afternoon out of the blue, *someone would have to be stupid to try anything.*

At least anything overt.

Davis had been here once before on a weapons buy. And he'd heard tell of good-filtering out of the base, goods to be purchased on the cheap, but he'd heard things like that on every single military base he'd had the misfortune to work near—which was too damn many.

He was a floater, never settling anywhere, not that anywhere was good enough to settle in. He hired one of the last phone services in the country—or it seemed that way, anyhow—instead of having some secretary man an office somewhere, and he occasionally toyed with getting a single cell number.

But phones were tricky nowadays, what with their GPS systems and the calls bouncing off various towers. Maybe they weren't so tricky in this part of Nevada because there weren't that many cell towers, so it was hard to pinpoint where someone was calling from, but get to Vegas and anyone with the right equipment could find him inside of an hour.

Not that he had done anything wrong.

Yet.

Here, in Nevada, anyway.

Still, he had Dirksen's cell, because Dirksen insisted on cells, but Davis hadn't purchased it, and he barely used it. At first, he didn't even keep it on, till Dirksen chewed him out royally. Now he had it on, but he didn't think about it.

Much.

The car bounced its way out of Hawthorne. He rounded a corner and crested a hill and there it was in front of him, the great lot of nothingness that made Nevada such a crazy useful state. In addition to the Hawthorne Ammunition Depot, there was Nellis Air Force Base, the Nevada Test Range, and Yucca Mountain, where the government was still trying to dump radioactive waste from other sites all over the United States.

He could understand it all. What other use would this place be? The communities were windswept and forlorn, what little building that went on seemed like kiddie toys placed upon the land.

If any place was designed to convince people they didn't belong on certain parts of the earth, then Nevada was that place.

Even the road, snaking through the dirt and dunes and ridges, looked like it had been glued onto an inhospitable surface. The road was the only bit of something in a whole lot of nothing.

Nothing…

Except an ancient van with a mattress bungee-corded to its roof, swaying precariously in the wind.

He could just make it out on the snaking road.

Hot damn if Dirksen wasn't right: you could see forever down here. Davis had no idea how far away from him she was, but he had found her, and he'd be able to see her as long as this road lasted, which, according to his GPS, was all the way to Vegas.

GPS, water, and food in the trunk, three separate laptops, clothing for a week, and of course, his extra weapons.

He kept his car stocked, and he was glad of it.

Because he was heading into no-man's land after a wobbly little van, and for the first time that day, he felt like this mission just might be a success.

— 12 —

There she was, in a Lexus SUV, no less. The woman from the casino, driving as if her life depended on it.

Moira was tempted to pass her just to prove she could. The woman wasn't speeding, probably afraid to overtax her car in this heat. Probably afraid to break down out here in all the nothingness, just like Moira was.

Only Moira wasn't afraid so much for herself. She'd survived worse than this place.

She was afraid for Kasey. The kid wouldn't last long in the heat. It wilted her because it was so dry, and Kasey was a Midwestern kid, born and bred in a place where heat was sticky and full of moisture. Moira'd been making her drink water from the moment they crossed the Rockies, although she hadn't focused on the water at the casino. Maybe she should've said no to the chocolate milk. Maybe she should've watched what Kasey was really eating.

But she hadn't been focused.

Just like she was having trouble focusing now.

What she really wanted to do was speed past the woman in the Lexus, then park sideways, blocking the middle of the highway, forcing the woman to stop.

Highway robbery. That would be fun. Pretending to be a highwayman of old, except instead of riding in on some kind of stallion, she

49

was coming in on a rusty minivan. She'd take the woman's keys and her money and her lovely expensive BlackBerry, and give her the keys to the minivan. She'd make the woman unload all of Kasey's things except the booster seat—Moira'd hook that up herself—and then she'd pack it all in the back, driving off, leaving the woman with the damn mattress, some clothes that didn't fit her, and a vehicle that worked but not nearly as well as a Lexus.

Although honestly, Moira wouldn't be doing it for the Lexus (except maybe for better air conditioning—and leather seats, soft as butter). Nope, she'd be doing it for the BlackBerry and that briefcase and the credit cards that she could pretend were hers for just one short instant. Maybe even the clothes—she'd drown in them most likely, but there'd be a few things she could wear.

For a short period—a few hours really, before everything got too hot to handle—she'd pretend it was all hers.

Not that this was a road you could steal anything on. All someone had to do was wait for you in Beatty, because Beatty was the only place that gave you a choice—head to Los Angeles via Death Valley or keep going on 95 until you got to Vegas.

Not that it was much of a choice. Certainly not one worth stealing over.

Still, who would suspect her? Hell, she could take the woman, kill her, dump the body and the van, and then turn around, drive north. She and Kasey, heading to Seattle, away from all this heat and dry and nothingness.

But the nothingness was the problem. There was no guarantee that Kasey would sleep through the shooting. Besides, it would take time to move Kasey's stuff—Moira could make do with nothing much, but Kasey loved her stuff. It was all she had.

Someone might drive by, maybe even stop for assistance as the two women moved boxes and dealt with the little girl. Someone would remember.

That was the problem with the van. It wasn't the right vehicle for a real crime, and this would be a real crime, not a stealth crime like the others had been.

Moira stepped on the gas. Screw it. She was going to pass the Lexus, maybe even smile at the woman, wave all friendly, just like Kasey had outside of Gary's house.

The woman would never know how close she came to a bullet in the head, how what she thought was a bad afternoon driving on a highway she didn't like was really a great afternoon because it was an afternoon where she was allowed to live, an afternoon where she got a second chance—when she hadn't even realized she had lost the first one.

Sometimes people were lucky.

And they never ever knew.

But Moira did.

And that was all that mattered.

— 13 —

Analyn couldn't wait any longer. She was driving herself crazy, checking her watch every fifteen minutes.

She'd left the fake canals and wandered through the casino, still stunned at the appeal of the games. She'd planned to go to the bank and get the five thousand in cash, but the clerk would remember her.

It wasn't until Analyn's fifth go-round in the casino that she figured out how to get the money so that no one would notice. But she didn't want to do it here; she felt exposed in the Venetian. She'd already spent too much time here.

So she walked through the indoor tunnels to New York New York, past more shopping, more restaurants, more slots—everything empty. The whole town looked lost without its tourists. She wondered what it had been like in the heyday before the recession, when everybody felt like they deserved an expensive vacation, all built on plastic.

She could afford the expensive vacation. She could afford a lot of things, but she didn't want them.

All she wanted was Kasey.

The tunnel threaded into New York New York. The casinos all had different layouts and color schemes, but they still sounded like casinos, with the electronic bursts of music, the subdued conversations lost in the thick carpeting. A waitress found Analyn almost immediately, offering her a drink from a tray of choices.

Analyn looked at the glasses, thinking how great a bourbon would taste right now. But a bourbon would be a bad idea. So would a beer. She'd feel it right away because she wasn't much of a drinker, and she'd just be drinking to numb herself for the wait.

Which was going poorly.

She looked at the new phone. No calls and it was only fifteen minutes since the last time she looked.

It felt like an hour.

So she wandered, in and out of slots, past a roulette wheel, to the teller's cage. The one consistency in every casino. They were gold, and they were barred, and it made Analyn feel like a criminal just to walk up to one.

She didn't even have to stand in line. There was one other man in front of a teller to her right. He was turning in chips.

She swallowed hard as she put her purse on the little ledge. "Can I get fifty-five hundred in chips?" she asked, fumbling for her black American Express.

"Sure," the teller said without looking up, as if she had gotten a request like this every day. Maybe she did. Maybe, when things were going well, she got one every hour. "How'd you want them?"

"Hmmm?" Analyn didn't understand the question. She looked toward the man. He was holding a plastic container that separated the chips into stacks. "In one of those little plastic things."

Then the clerk did look up. She smiled as she did so. Analyn could read that expression. Tourist. Newbie.

Rube.

"I'm sorry, ma'am," the teller said. "Do you want hundred-dollar chips, five-hundred-dollar chips, twenty-dollar chips—?"

"Whatever's easier," Analyn said.

The clerk frowned. Apparently that wasn't the right answer. Apparently, Analyn was supposed to have a preference.

The clerk took the credit card, ran it, and then had Analyn sign. She did, with a little flourish. While she ran the pen across that thin slip of paper that would buy her girl back, she watched out of the corner of her eye as the clerk counted out chips in various colors, stacking them on one of those little plastic thingies.

Then she ran her fake fingernail across the top, counting it out for Analyn, explaining which color signified what denomination of money.

So easy. So ridiculously easy.

Her mouth was dry.

She took the little plastic thingie away. It was heavier than she expected. She stopped at an empty blackjack table and caught her breath.

Then she looked at her phone. Another fifteen minutes. That was it. Just fifteen minutes.

Her life, in fifteen minute segments.

Kasey wasn't even due here for another four hours, minimum.

Analyn sighed. Then she looked at the roulette table. That was the only game she had any idea at all how to play.

She wandered over to it, set her chips in front of a chair, and sat down. Then she carefully picked out a five hundred, setting it on the table proper. She'd play until it was gone.

That should take an hour or two.

She hoped.

And of course, she was wrong.

— 14 —

Only ten dollars in tips. Jenny slid out of the car, hating that she had to park on the street. Of course, Gary hadn't moved the Jeep even though she had asked him to. They had a perfectly good garage, and if he didn't want to use it, she did. She wanted to park inside, get out of the car, and go through the interior door to the kitchen, because she wouldn't have to be on her feet any longer.

There was nothing worse than waiting tables in a recession in a town that hadn't brought her a lot of business anyway. Standing around waiting for people to come in was worse than running your tail off.

She gathered her purse and got out of the car. The heat was worse in the afternoon. The light even shimmered like it did in the movies, just before the hero passed out on the desert floor. Somehow she hadn't seen marriage like this. Somehow she thought it would be more glamorous, especially married to a guy in the military. They'd travel to interesting places, and she'd make them a home.

Instead, they ended up here, which was, she had to admit, interesting during the first year—she'd never met people like these, people who decorated their yards with empty bombshells, for heaven's sake. Tough people, people who had seen it all and lived to tell about it.

But the novelty had worn off, and the heat was bringing her down. The heat and the monotony. Tell her the day of the week and she would be able to tell you who'd be in the restaurant. Today was no different. The only thing that was unusual about it was that the strangers passing through—what few of them there were—happened to be women. Mostly the one-timers who stopped at the casino were men or older married couples.

Everyone else drove a truck—either cargo or delivery. The only thing that differentiated them from each other was their clothing. The delivery guys actually wore a uniform, poor things.

Not that she should say anything. She wore a uniform too, which smelled of grease at the end of the day whether the restaurant was busy or not.

She let herself in the front door because she didn't want to walk the extra distance through the garage. Her feet hurt worse than usual today. She needed new shoes. This pair had cracks on the interior that were irritating her feet.

Gary told her he'd have money soon, but it wasn't soon enough. She was getting tired of living hand to mouth.

The only problem was that she didn't see any other choice—especially now that she was beginning to realize that Gary's promises of extra money weren't worth the air he used to make them.

The house was dark and smelled funny. She sniffed, trying to figure out the scent. Almost like someone had been sick, but that wasn't quite it. There was a metallic tinge to it.

Maybe the air conditioning was on the fritz. God knows everything else was.

Except the TV in the kitchen. She could hear the *Sports Center* guys rambling on about that days' news. It said a lot about her marriage that she didn't like sports and she knew who the *Sports Center* guys were.

She set her purse on the coffee table even though she had told Gary repeatedly that the coffee table was to remain clean. She didn't care today. Today, she'd stood for hours and only made ten bucks over and above her paltry wages. Today she could break as many rules as she wanted.

"Gar?" she called.

Dammit, was he in the back yard under the sprinkler again? Didn't he know they could be fined for using the sprinkler in the middle of a hot summer day?

She walked into the kitchen. The smell was worse here and someone had moved the place mats. Then she glanced at the TV. Something had spattered all over the *Sports Center* guys. She peered at it, and nearly tripped.

She looked down and saw—Jesus! Gary! She wasn't sure if she said that out loud, then realized she probably hadn't. Her breath was coming in short gasps. She crouched. His eyes were half open, and there was a stain running down her cupboards. It would take forever to get that out. Blood. Blood. Oh, Christ.

His right hand was clutching a drawer handle, his left to one side. His chest was open, and there was blood all over the floor.

She had stepped in it. In her crummy shoes. She backed away as she stood up, nearly losing her balance. Shitshitshitshit. She grabbed the phone, the landline she wanted to get rid of, the one that Gary insisted on keeping, and she punched 911 and when they asked her what her emergency was she thought it wasn't her emergency it was Gary's and he hadn't called and someone shot him and ohmygod he was dead people with their eyes open were dead weren't they and the 911 operator asked again what her emergency was and she said calmer than she thought she could, not that she was trying to be calm, she said, "He's dead, I think," and then she sat in her kitchen chair and stared at him, wondering if he had known how unhappy she was with him, how much she had stopped believing in him, and if that lack of belief had killed him even though part of her brain (the logical part) knew it couldn't happen that way.

She stared at him and she willed him to get up because no matter what, Gary handled the emergencies. He couldn't be the emergency. She didn't want him to be an emergency and leave her here in this horrible place with bombs in her front yard for godsake and a dead man in her kitchen, a dead husband in her kitchen—shot.

Shot.

Shot.

She looked around. God, she was sitting here and someone had shot Gary and that someone could still be here and she bolted—bolted! She'd never done that in her life—out the front door, standing on the sidewalk with the phone in one hand and her purse in the other, even though she didn't remember grabbing it.

The 911 operator was still talking and in the distance she heard sirens and it was really very hot and she went to her car, knowing better than to drive away, but wanting to be away, and she sat inside with the door open and her feet on the grass, staring at the blood on her shoes, as the sirens got closer and closer, waiting for them to arrive and someone to tell her what to do.

— 15 —

It had started out as a speck, just something black in her rearview mirror. Then it morphed into a sedan, the kind that should be slow, but wasn't. Modified? Like the cops did? Adding an engine with more horsepower because he was gaining on her faster than he should.

Either that or Moira's speedometer was off. But she hadn't had trouble passing the woman in the Lexus. She'd left that fancy car in the dust.

She'd even waved at the woman as she went by, grinning the entire time. The woman had smiled and waved back with something like relief, probably thinking at least there was someone nice out here to turn to if her big fancy car broke down in the heat.

Moira glanced in her rearview. The black sedan was several miles behind her, not that it mattered. You could see everything for miles and miles and miles. If someone was tailing you, you'd know it—or at least suspect it.

And she'd been suspecting it for a while now.

Although she was probably paranoid. After all, where would he turn off? There were no side roads. There was nowhere to go. Anyone who got on 95 stayed on 95 until they got where they were going.

For all she knew, the sedan belonged to another business traveler like the woman, someone who was cursing their hours on this road, and wishing there was an easier way north-to-south from Fallon to Vegas.

There was only one way to find out. Moira would stop in Tonopah. If he was still behind her after that, then she'd assume he was following her.

Not that she would take evasive action.

If the sedan was part of the state police, then he would have to pull her over, and she'd have to be all friendly.

Mostly, she'd have to keep him out of her purse.

She glanced at it.

She should've got rid of the silencer. But those things were expensive and finding the right one for her gun wasn't the easiest thing in the world.

The gun was explainable—woman alone with a kid on the desolate roadways of North America—but the silencer, that was serious business, used by someone with intent.

Her fingers itched. She wanted to reach into the purse now—in fact, she could picture herself leaning over, fumbling in the purse while she struggled to keep her eyes on the road, grabbing the silencer, and then rolling down her window, tossing the damn thing out.

But she knew better. Because if he—and why the hell did she assume the driver was a he? The only other person on this road with her so far had been a woman—was a cop and he saw something bounce out of her van, he'd stop and take a look, and see the silencer and *know*.

So she was better off flirting and looking sunburned and tired (hell, she *was* sunburned and tired) and then pleading family in Vegas and heading off.

There was family in Vegas—Analyn, waiting—so that wouldn't be a lie. There wouldn't be a lot of lies in what Moira said, none really. Even if he (she, dammit!) asked her about Gary, she'd say she saw him and that Kasey said good-bye to him on the way out. True, all true. It just left out the important part—the gunshots, the way he slid down to the floor, the surprise people always seemed to have when she ended up shooting them as if they hadn't expected, living the way they lived, to die that way, at the end of someone else's gun.

Dumb fucks.

Kasey stirred in the backseat. "We there yet?" she mumbled.

"No, baby," Moira said. "Go back to sleep."

"Need to pee."

For real this time.

"Can you wait? We'll be in the next town in ten minutes." Give or take. But the kid didn't need to know that. Kasey couldn't tell time yet—not the smaller units, anyway. Hours she had. Minutes were still beyond her.

"I guess." She sounded sleepy.

"I'll wake you when we get there," Moira said.

"'Kay," Kasey said.

Moira glanced in the rearview, this time looking at Kasey, with more than the usual concern. The air conditioning was working, but it was struggling with this heat. But Kasey's skin was its normal color, her cheeks the kind of rosy only little girls had. Her gaze met Moira's in the mirror and she smiled a tired little smile.

She was okay, so far.

A few more hours. She had to stay healthy for just a few more hours.

Eternity, really.

At least in this desert.

Moira turned her gaze back to the red dirt nothingness in front of her, and willed the van to Tonopah.

She needed a stop too, if only to get out of the sun.

And to see if that sedan would wait for her to get back onto 95.

— 16 —

Zane's fingers hovered over the keyboard. Great visuals on the front of the house. Great scary visuals.

For three weeks, he'd come in, watched that house that looked like every other house on the block, and then he'd left. He'd made note of people coming and going and listened to the dullest fuckin' phone calls he'd ever heard in his life, and then he'd gone back to the room in Hawthorne's cruddy roadside motel and slept like a dead person, only to get up and do it all over again.

Except today when Davis—the asshole—called him in (actually Dirksen called him because Davis had figured out that Zane wouldn't take orders from him. The asshole) and then fled like the cops were after him.

And maybe they were, judging by what was going on out there.

First, that Jenny lady gets home. That's normal about this time in the afternoon. He didn't even think much of it, because she always pulls up out front, always bitches to the Gary guy that he hasn't moved his damn Jeep, and he tells her it's his house, he can park where he wants—usually saying all of that loudly on the front lawn when he could just as easily get into the Jeep and drive it into the garage or move it so she can park in the garage. After all, that Jenny lady had a point, she did work on her feet all day while he sat on his ass making phone call after phone call setting up his stupid deal.

62

Zane usually watched the fight from his own picture window, hovering behind the curtains like Lyman taught him. Lyman, he was nice, not like Davis the Asshole who thought everyone was incompetent except him.

Davis, who lost the target somehow.

Zane had never seen him so panicked.

But nothing was normal this afternoon. Except the Jenny lady getting home. Zane had braced himself for the fight or for one of them to go slamming out of the house like they usually did after the fight, but that hadn't happened.

He had waited for it and when he was about to give up, the Jenny lady ran out of the house like something was after her, terrified, holding the phone and her purse like she didn't even know what she had in her hands.

He expected the Gary guy to come out after her, and he hadn't. The door just stayed open and she went for the car, and that was when Zane realized she was leaving footprints—and who the hell left footprints when they ran *from* their house?

So he went to the computer and zoomed in and realized the footprints were dark. He zoomed some more, and damn if that wasn't blood.

He'd seen blood before, more of it than Davis the Asshole would've believed, and he knew what bloody footprints—wet bloody footprints—looked like and he was seeing it now.

Davis had really fucked up, if someone was dead in that house. He hadn't said anything to Zane, not that he would, Davis thinking Zane was an idiot.

Maybe that was what he meant by losing the lead. Maybe Gary had done something, because Gary wasn't the sharpest tool in the box, and then zoomed off—only Gary would've taken the Jeep, wouldn't he?

Except that Davis'd been really clear. The lead was a woman, and the Gary guy and that Jenny lady were fighting all the time. So maybe Gary did something to someone inside and got into a car with a woman and took off.

Zane would believe it. He'd believe damn near anything, the way those two fought.

He always felt bad about it, too, since he went to the restaurant in the casino a lot. Used to be he'd go because he liked the food, and then he thought it was totally cool to be waited on by a woman who thought she was just some waitress and he knew all kinds of stuff about her, like what time she got home and what she wore to bed (gotta love those cameras) and the look on her face when she left the house every morning.

But he'd never seen a look like today's, and then she uses the house phone and her voice comes in really clear and she's saying someone's dead, and that's when Zane picks up his cell and pauses.

He's supposed to contact Davis, but Davis is going after some lead. So Zane clutches the phone a minute longer and that's when she runs out and that's when he realizes all about the blood and that's when he's making sure he has the video because he's going to send it to Dirksen who is, after all, the guy who pays his salary.

He gets the e-mail together and then the first cop car shows up, squealing down the road and parking haphazardly in front of the house.

"Fuck," Zane said and then "Fuck" again as another cop car shows up and another and another, and it looks like the whole Hawthorne police department is parked in the middle of the road on a street he's supposed to be monitoring in front of a house where a woman just fled with blood on her shoes, and if he didn't do something soon, he'd be fired, and he wasn't sure what to do because he's not the brains of the operation and he knows it, and so he hesitates one more second, and then he scrolled through his contacts until he found Dirksen.

Zane winced as the phone completed the call. This might lose him his job, too, but he needed to know what to do.

"I told you not to call this number," Dirksen said.

"There's something going down, and I'm the only one here," Zane said. His voice shook. He hadn't wanted it to shake, but it did, goddammit, and he sounded like a kid, just like Davis the Asshole always called him.

"What's going down?" Dirksen asked, and Zane let out a small breath. Because if he'd done wrong, Dirksen would've yelled at him some more and Dirksen didn't.

So Zane told him about the woman and the shoes and the blood—
"I sent the video. You should have it in your e-mail now"—and then he
mentioned the cops, and Dirksen cursed, a string of words that didn't
belong together but sounded amazingly cool, and Zane would've tried
to memorize them if he wasn't so terrified himself.

"Gimme a minute," Dirksen said after he'd finished swearing, and
Zane could hear the pings and bongs of a computer.

While he waited, he looked out the window, saw the cops milling, a
few going into the house, and someone stopping them, and then another
guy, on the phone—probably to the state police, or maybe the military
police, considering that Gary guy was military—and they all loitered except one guy who was crouched in front of poor old Jenny, who looked
like she was crying now.

"Fuck," Dirksen said, but not loud, like he was talking to himself.
Then he said, "Get over there and find out what's going on."

"Davis said I'm not supposed to leave the house, that we screw up if
anyone sees us."

"Well, screw up then," Dirksen said, "because you're not going to
learn anything in there."

"What'm'I supposed to say? That I'm watching the house and—"

"Shit, kid, I don't know. You're supposed to be the brains of the operation, and you're asking me?"

He wasn't the brains, he knew it, but he was the computer guy, and
everybody thought the computer guy was the brains, so maybe that was
what Dirksen meant. Because to Zane, the brains of the operation was
always the guy in charge, which meant Davis or maybe Dirksen, and
they told him what to do and where to stand and when to do it.

"I'm blown if I do that," Zane said.

"I think the operation's over, kid," Dirksen said, "at least this part of
it. So go, insinuate yourself, be the nosy neighbor, and then report back
to me. You got that?"

"Yeah." He could do that. He could be the nosy neighbor. Hell, he
was the nosy neighbor. "I'll call back as soon as I know something."

"You do that," Dirksen said like it was the stupidest thing he'd ever heard, and then he hung up.

Zane stared at the phone for a minute. Dirksen scared him more than all the cops did.

Then he took a deep breath, hitched up his pants, ran his hand through his hair like he'd just woken up, and let himself outside.

By the time he got across the street, he already had a role for himself, the teenage son of the new neighbors who spent his afternoon watching the street because he couldn't find a job, and he didn't want to be like everybody else in this stinkin' town and enlist.

He swaggered to the nearest cop car, his stomach jumping, and hovered, unable to say even a shaky hello.

No one noticed him, but he could see inside the house, cops crowding the kitchen, someone else pointing, and he could hear the jagged jumpy conversation the cop was having with Jenny and the guy on the phone, saying this could be big, they'd been watching this guy for a while.

Zane shoved his thumbs in his pockets and watched. If they noticed him, fine. If they didn't, he'd still learn things.

And as he stood, another stranger joined him, then another. The cop cars drew observers like flies.

He felt better then, like he might succeed. Like Dirksen wouldn't be pissed at him forever.

Besides, he had to remember. Whatever happened here happened on Davis's watch, not his. And if something went wrong, he could always blame Davis, instead of letting the blame fall on himself.

— 17 —

He stood in the kitchen and studied the body. Detective Douglas Cahill never thought he'd see another body, not like this one. Sure, he had domestics and the occasional drunken buddy murder, but this—this looked serious.

LA kinda serious. The kind he left behind.

He hitched his pants over his stomach. Fifty pounds heavier than he'd been when he left the LAPD, a hundred heavier than he'd been when he started there. The Hawthorne P.D. had regulations about staying fit, but unlike LA, Hawthorne didn't enforce them, especially with guys like Cahill, whom the Hawthorne P.D. felt they needed to have.

A real-life police detective, the kind that worked homicides in a city where homicides happened every day instead of once or twice a year. The kind of experience a department needed just in case there was a Big One, as the chief of police here in tiny Hawthorne said when he hired Cahill.

Not that I'm expecting a Big One, the chief added. *It's just every community gets one sooner or later.*

Cahill had been banking on later. He'd left LA like so many did, with a little dirt on his shield and more exhaustion than he wanted to think about. He wanted somewhere quiet to spend the next ten years until he retired—and when he retired, he didn't want to "retire" as in needing to work security somewhere to supplement his income. He wanted the whole nine yards—a nice house, some travel, and no work, not ever again.

He had house here—paid off, using only a percentage of the money from his LA house (sold when the market was at its peak)—and enough stashed away to retire now, plus buy a place somewhere south, Vegas maybe or Phoenix or Florida. Not LA again.

He was done with LA.

Or so he thought.

Until now.

"What're you seeing that I'm not?" asked Rosemary Brett, his partner—as if cops needed partners here. But really, she was always riding along with him, to hear the stories and to learn by osmosis. The chief hoped she'd be lead detective when Cahill was gone, hoped she'd handle the Big One when it came.

But she wasn't going to.

Because the Big One was here now. He was looking at it.

"Pro job," he said, keeping his voice flat.

Brett peered at the body. She was good; she didn't move toward it like so many of the other hick cops had, enough that he'd had to warn them away.

"Shots are in the chest," she said. "I thought pros went for the face."

"What'd they teach you if you have to unload your weapon?" he asked. Asking her those questions, the kind that facilitated learning, had become reflex for him.

"Handicap if possible," she said, the answer clearly reflex as well.

"And if you have to put him down?" he asked.

"Shoot for the widest surface," she said.

"Which is…?"

"The torso," she said, and frowned. "But this is close-range. Why not go for the face?"

He shrugged. "Face shots hide identity. This is Gary Storvick's house, and that's his body, and he was discovered by his own wife. Identity would be easy to determine even if the face was gone."

He sighed, glanced at ESPN still running on the TV, the blowback from the first shot still spattered all over the screen. The sound was on low, and he didn't know if Storvick had done that or if one of the first responders had turned it down.

"The other reason for face shots is hatred," he said. "You want to obliterate the son of a bitch, torso shots ain't good enough. You gotta demolish *them*, who they are. And that's the face."

"So you don't think this is personal," Brett said.

"Didn't say that."

"But you said face shots were personal."

"I said they came from hatred. You can kill someone you know, maybe even for personal reasons, and not hate them." He glanced around. So far as he could tell—and he'd have to ask the wife to be sure—nothing was out of place. "This is a particularly cold-blooded shoot. The door wasn't jimmied, there's no sign of robbery, and he's in the kitchen, with the TV on, no weapon in his hand, no signs of a struggle. He came in here with his pal and his pal shot him. End of story."

"Twice," Rosemary said. "Shot him twice. Isn't that an indicator of hatred?"

"Caution." He nodded toward the spatter. "The first shot probably would've killed him, but slowly. The shooter wanted to make the death go a little quicker. Again, the opposite of hatred. Cold-blooded."

"You seem sure of yourself." That voice came from the living room. Cahill turned. One of the street cops—what was his name? Watson? Wylie? Wicker?—leaned against the door jamb.

"I'm sure you're contaminating evidence," Cahill said. "You want to stand up like a man?"

Whatsisname flushed. He hated Cahill, called him Big Shot, and Detective, with a sarcastic emphasis on the *dee*.

"Shouldn't the coroner determine which shot was the kill shot?" Whatsisname asked.

"He will, I'm sure," Cahill said. "But from where I'm standing, this is a pro job, maybe even contract. Cold, quick, and relatively easy. Our shooter's probably long gone."

"You don't even know time of death," Whatsisname said.

Cahill gave a tight little smile. He wasn't going to fight with a doo-fus. He decided not to point out that the pooled blood wasn't tacky yet, not even on the edges, and that rigor hadn't started. This was a fresh corpse. Fresh corpses had a look, a near-life appearance even if they'd bled white. This guy looked fresh as fresh could be.

No brass either, and it didn't look like the shooter cleaned up. Judging from the holes, the shooter used a .38. Unusual gun these days, popular a long time ago. Cahill'd seen a lot of them in LA, but only because they were cheap. Again, though, he'd have to wait for the coroner's verdict.

But he did know this: the shooter was cautious. No footprints in the blood, even though Cahill would wager that the shooter waited to see the victim bleed out.

But Cahill didn't say any of that. He didn't need to defend himself or his assumptions, based as they were on twenty-five years of Los Angeles corpses, sometimes daily. Hell, he'd probably seen more homicides than the every coroner in the state of Nevada—if you discounted Vegas's coroner, of course.

"You guys wanna let me do my job?" he asked, making sure there was an edge in his voice.

"Looks like you're just staring," Whatsisname said.

Cahill turned toward him. Whatsisname was still leaning on the door jamb. Cahill glared at him until Whatsisname stood upright.

Then Whatsisname straightened the shirt of his uniform, nodded once, and walked back through the living room, probably forgetting to avoid walking on the wife's bloody footprints.

At the moment, Cahill didn't care. At the moment, he just wanted to study the corpse.

"You want me to leave, too?" Brett asked.

"Make sure the yahoos don't contaminate my scene any more than they have," Cahill said.

She nodded, then followed Whatsisname out of the kitchen. Cahill crouched. The vic's chest was a shiny mass of blood, shirt sticking to his skin. There was a phone attached to the vic's belt, and a bulge—phone shaped—in the front pocket of his jeans.

Two phones? And a landline right next to the TV, also covered with spatter.

Cahill'd kept an eye on Storvick out of sheer doggedness. Storvick had come into Hawthorne, all bluster and talk, and had brought some undesirables with him. Cahill had expected Storvick to get into trouble. Just hadn't expected him to get dead.

The double cells—if, indeed, that's what he was looking at—were the best indicator of trouble besides the corpse himself.

"What're you into?" Cahill muttered.

He had a hunch it wouldn't take too long to find out.

— 18 —

Tonopah looked like it must've been someplace once. A big old brick courthouse rose out of the dirt like a castle; a matching schoolhouse wasn't too far away. From a distance, the entire town looked like an oasis in the desert, but as Moira pulled up into the city streets, crisscrossed by railroad tracks, she noted a distinct lack of care.

Dusty walls, broken windows, abandoned storefronts. And not newly abandoned either, not from the modern recession, but long-ago abandoned, like no one had inhabited those buildings for decades, maybe longer.

Her stomach clenched. She'd promised Kasey a stop here, and Kasey was getting insistent. Child bladders weren't very forgiving, and Moira'd learned that the hard way. She couldn't expect Kasey to wait too much longer.

The highway curved, and on the curve was a combination grocery store, restaurant, and single-pump gas station, the kind that only seemed to exist in the West. She pulled in, grabbed her purse, then got out. The heat seemed worse here, more vivid, as if there was nothing between the sun and her skin.

She opened the back door, unlatched Kasey from the booster seat, and helped her down. Kasey still clutched the Barbie, but this time, Moira took it from her and put it back on the booster. She didn't want to lose that doll in this town and have to come back.

"She'll be okay," Moira said.

Kasey gave the doll a worried look, but didn't complain, which meant that the bladder was closer to bursting than Moira thought.

"Let's go," Moira said.

She took Kasey's hand and led her to the dusty glass door without even locking the van. Let someone steal what was inside, she dared them. Not that there was much. The only things she had of value were in her purse or belonged to that warm hand clutched around hers.

A bell rang as she stepped inside. The air was cooler here and it was dark compared to that sunlight. Moira had to blink a few times before she could even see the counter.

A woman stood behind it—a girl, really, skinny and black-haired, maybe twenty-one at the outside.

"Bathroom?" Moira asked.

The girl pointed, and Moira dragged Kasey past a pile of boxes to the bathroom, which was cleaner than she expected. Kasey headed to the toilet as Moira locked the door. While the little girl took care of business, Moira looked in the cracked mirror.

God, she was sunburned, face like a flaming neon sign. She splashed cold water on her skin, and that helped some. She'd buy more sunscreen here and she'd use some of it, maybe some with lotion. She could afford to give up a few of her precious dollars, since she'd be getting more in Vegas.

For the first time in years, she hadn't planned her cash right. She had more than enough money, but she always traveled with enough cash so that she didn't have to use an ATM on a job. And kids were extremely expensive. She had no idea how parents did it.

Kasey finished, flushed, and made her way to the sink. She needed help reaching the taps, but she cleaned up good. She always did.

Moira sometimes wondered how this kid ended up being so good, and then answered her own question. She'd seen kids like Kasey in the system, kids who figured out the best way to survive was to hunker down and not make waves, to take care of themselves instead of expecting someone else to do it for them.

Like Moira had been.

She handed Kasey some paper towels, then made her wait while Moira took care of things. While she sat, she realized this was the place to get rid of the silencer. Not this bathroom, but this town. Who'd look here? And she could buy another in Vegas if she needed one. When she needed one.

They left the bathroom. A boy/man had joined the girl/woman behind the counter. Moira's eyes had adjusted and she saw what she'd missed, the baby carrier on the counter, with a girl—judging by the pink—not more than three months old inside.

"Yours?" Moira asked, playing the friendly traveling mom.

The girl/woman smiled, a soft, sweet look, possessive and proud at the same time. The boy glanced at the baby and put a protective hand on her chubby knee.

"She's darling," Moira said.

"Yes," the girl said softly. "I don't normally bring her to work. I don't want her growing up in no store, but I don't like to be away from her, neither."

"I know," Moira said. "It's hard, especially when they're young."

She glanced at Kasey, who was eyeing a row of candy bars. Moira grabbed a cold bottle of water from one of the refrigerator cases, waved the bottle at the girl, and said, "I'm going to get other things, but I want her to start on this."

The girl nodded. The boy glowered and punched in the amount on the computer, which was the only modern thing in the place.

Moira turned the top, and handed the water to Kasey. "Drink slow," she said.

Kasey nodded, then wandered down the next aisle.

"Can you keep an eye on her?" Moira asked. "I have to get something from the van."

"Sure," the girl said.

"If you pay for that," the boy said.

"Garth," the girl hissed.

"It's okay," Moira said. She put two dollars on the counter. "That enough?"

"Yeah," the boy said, reaching inside for change. Moira deliberately left it behind. She went out the door, back into the hot sun, then walked around behind the van, and surveyed the area.

Not as many windows in that store as she would have thought—as would've been practical, really. Just the front door and two front windows. Everything else was hidden by the red brick that seemed like it was ubiquitous here. Obviously the store had been some other kinda business once upon a time.

She glanced around the side. She could get to the Dumpster without anyone seeing her from the store. She looked across the street. Another brick building, this one advertising an insurance agency with a faded closed sign on the door.

No other cars, not even the sedan. Maybe she'd been wrong. Maybe it hadn't been following her after all.

Or maybe it hadn't gotten to Tonopah yet. Hard to tell distance in this damn desert.

She should've parked on a side street. Shoulda woulda coulda.

Better to take care of the silencer now.

She glanced at the door and the silent street. She only had a few minutes before the girl/woman would think she'd abandoned Kasey.

Moira slipped around the side of the van and headed toward the Dumpster. One quick movement, and she'd be done. Then she'd go back to being friendly traveling mom, who needed sunscreen, a snack, and just a few more hours to get her to Las Vegas.

— 19 —

Davis slipped out of his car. He eased the door closed so that he could barely hear it latch. It wasn't shut tight, but it didn't matter. If there was anyone alive in this one-horse town, they were welcome to steal whatever they found. They probably wouldn't know what to do with it when they got it, and he'd catch them. No one would be able to outsmart him, not here.

He had parked behind an abandoned brick building that had once housed an insurance agency. Through his mirrors, he could see the store and the van. He'd shown up after the woman and the little girl had gone inside, and he debated walking in, maybe cornering the woman, asking her a few questions.

He wasn't sure he wanted to keep following her if she wasn't his lead. He hated it out here, worse than he hated Hawthorne. If he could talk to her, he'd know if she was the contact, just by the way she acted. If she was an old girlfriend, she'd be angry that Gary Storvick threw her out of the house. If it was a paternity thing, she'd want someone to talk to.

If she needed more money, she wouldn't say no to the cash Davis was willing to give her for her crap-ass information.

Of course, if she said no to any of that stuff, or wasn't angry, or was skittish just when he came into the store, he'd know she was the contact,

76

and he'd follow her all the way to hell and gone, which—judging by the landscape around him—was exactly where she was going.

He had a little speech all prepared, something about following her distinctive van all the way from Hawthorne, and he'd be happy to help her secure that mattress better, when she walked out of the store alone. She went to the back of the van and looked around like she was making sure no one watched her.

That caught his interest, and the fact that she didn't have the little girl gave him a whole new plan. He could get information the old-fashioned way. He could threaten it out of her, maybe even threaten the little girl's life. That would make any woman give up needed information.

He walked around the building, his sneakers silent on the pavement. No traffic since he stopped. The town was deader than the highway. He wondered how the store even stayed in business.

The woman made her way around the van and headed to the side of the store. No windows there, at least that he could see.

Even better.

He moved quietly, following her. She stepped into a side street. A Dumpster had been pushed against the wall of the building—no windows, no doors—and no windows across the street either. What was it with this place?

She was rooting in her purse, looking for something as she stood in front of the Dumpster.

Davis approached, blocking her way to the van. He'd been hoping for an alley. In an alley he could trap her. But this would do as well.

"You know Gary Storvick," he said.

She looked up, her face beet-red. But not from surprise or shock or embarrassment. Sunburn. And her gaze was flat.

"I *knew* Gary Storvick," she said, and pulled out a gun.

— 20 —

She shot him.

He stumbled backwards, and fell to one knee. She'd never seen him before, but she knew who he was.

The guy in the sedan.

He was a big guy, middle-aged, wearing clothes one size too big. As he fell, she realized he wore the clothes to hide how trim he was.

He toppled sideways, landed hard, but didn't grunt.

She waited a half second, wondering if she'd hear that bell from the store's door. But she didn't. They hadn't heard the gun.

Of course not. She hadn't removed the silencer.

She kept the gun in one hand and moved toward him. He watched her, eyes bright. She could never tell if guys this close to death actually saw anything, and she didn't want to ask.

She shot him again—torso, not far from the first shot, and that did it. He was dead. Eyes empty, mouth slack. One minute there, the next gone. Funny that. This guy went quicker than Gary. Maybe her first shot'd been cleaner. Or maybe this guy was just ready to die.

She shoved the gun back into her purse, then pulled out the travel pack of Kleenex she always carried, took a few tissues, and put them in her palms.

Then she walked over to him and bent down. Yep, dead. Pupils fixed, no faking that. His pupils should've moved if he was playing dead.

Hell, anyone with half a brain could play dead with his eyes closed.

She grabbed his left wrist with her right hand. His right wrist was under his leg. She used her foot to move his right arm. His body rolled slightly. She grabbed his right wrist and tugged him toward the Dumpster.

Fucker had to weigh two hundred, two-ten, almost too much for her to drag, especially dead. Death/unconsciousness/drunk, all seemed to add another fifty pounds.

She didn't care. She had to get him out of sight, not because she was worried about the police—she wasn't. If Tonopah had a police department, it had to be small—but because she didn't want Kasey to see him and ask questions.

She dragged and leaned and dragged, sweat pouring down her sunburned face, stinging as it went. The body left a trail. Looked like slime, even though she knew it was blood, glistening. She managed to get him behind the Dumpster, but didn't cover him with anything. Better to leave him there. When the couple came out to dump their trash, they'd find him.

She dropped his wrists, and shoved the Kleenex in her pockets. Then she looked for her purse. She'd dropped it when she pulled out the gun, and fortunately the purse was far from the blood trail.

The damn blood trail. She didn't want Kasey to see that either. She kicked gravel over it, covering enough of it so that it wasn't pointing right at him.

Then she checked her shoes. Some dirt, a little blood. She grabbed her purse, then went to the back of the van, opened it, reached inside, and took out a garbage bag. She shoved the shoes inside, grabbed a pair of flip-flops she'd hoped to never wear again, and slipped them on.

She closed the van, wiped her hands on her jeans, slung her purse over her shoulder, and went inside the store.

The girl/woman smiled at her, but frowned at the same time. "Everything okay?"

For a minute, Moira thought she'd heard the shot. Then she realized Moira had probably taken longer than the girl expected. Kasey was sitting on a barstool behind the counter, sipping the water and staring at the baby like the baby was a Barbie doll.

"Broke a strap on my shoe," Moira said. "Had to switch them out."

She lifted a foot with the flip-flop, just in case the girl had noticed.

"I hate that," the girl said.

The boy stood close to the baby as if he thought Kasey was going to hurt it.

"You got 50 SPF?" Moira asked.

"30," the girl said. "That's all we can do. You might want some aloe, too."

"I do want aloe," Moira said, and walked to the aisle the girl indicated. She grabbed the sunscreen and the aloe, as well as more tissues. Then she picked up some Oreos and another bottle of water, a big one, one that should take them to Vegas.

She piled it all on the counter, watched as the boy rang it up. Probably a big haul for them these days.

He gave her a total and she paid with cash, wishing she didn't have to. Paper held fingerprints too, although cash was pretty dirty, a thousand different fingerprints over time. Plus they'd have to use some special process to get the prints off.

She was careful not to give him any coins. Coins were easier to print. And she didn't touch anything except the stuff she bought.

He bagged it for her in an old plastic grocery sack. She wrapped it around her wrist, thought of how sturdy wrists were—just a half second loss of focus—then smiled at Kasey.

"You ready to go, babe?" she asked.

Kasey nodded and got off the stool. She scampered to Moira's side.

"Say good-bye," Moira said.

Kasey smiled and waved, looking not at the couple, but at the baby.

"Bye," she said, and this time she meant it. "Bye-bye."

— 21 —

Cahill knew the wife, casually of course. He knew damn near everyone in Hawthorne casually. Figured in a town this small it was his duty to keep an eye on the locals.

He stood a few yards from his car and watched the woman, trying to get her measure. She'd been crying. Her shoes were bloody and they left prints. She was leaning against her car, not even noticing how heat-baked it was in the sun, and she was staring at her own house as if she hadn't seen it before.

Frankly, he'd expected more problems like this one when he moved here. The thing LA taught you was how much could go wrong. If you looked at the world like one giant problem waiting to happen, you postponed a lot of heartache.

Hawthorne had its problems, and more it didn't even realize. First, it had the Ammunition Depot. Lots of weapons came in and out of this place, most of them decommissioned, some experimental. But the longer he lived here the more he realized the military had that place under control. If someone wanted to deal weapons out of Hawthorne, they'd be caught and locked up for just having the thought.

The Depot was at risk for other things—unplanned explosions, terrible accidents, leaking toxins. But, he'd learned, explosions were never "unplanned" even if they took the military by surprise, accidents didn't happen even if someone died on base, and toxins never leaked no matter what the locals said.

He couldn't—and didn't—worry about the Depot.

He worried about the transients.

Hawthorne had its share, being the best stop on Highway 95 between Fallon and Vegas. People stayed here when their cars broke down, had lunch here on the way to Vegas, panicked here when they realized that the whole lotta nothing they just drove through was a whole lotta something compared to what was facing them south of town.

Cahill kept an eye on the transients and the shady locals, like Gary Storvick, who made too many promises, talked too much about big money, and had too much of an attitude problem for a guy who was supposed to be career military.

Cahill sighed, wiped the sweat off his face, and headed to the wife. He used to love these interviews. People in the middle of a crisis never thought about what they were going to say. But he'd learned to hate these interviews in a small town.

Because next week or the week after, Jenny Storvick would be back at the casino serving coffee with a side of surly, and she wouldn't be happy to see him. He wouldn't be happy to see her, either.

It had always been easier to harass witnesses when he knew he probably wouldn't ever see them again.

So he decided to do his best Andy Griffith, at least to start. Friendly small-town sheriff (not that he was a sheriff, but still), a nice guy, someone she could confide in.

And if that didn't work, then she better look out.

"Ma'am," he said as he approached, touching his forehead as if he'd forgotten his hat. "You want to go in the garage? I'll bet it's cooler in there."

She shook her head. Her face was mottled, but he couldn't tell if it was from crying or from the heat.

"I don't want to go inside that place ever again," she said.

He didn't point out that the garage wasn't the house, and that she'd have to go back inside to get her stuff, if nothing else.

"When we're done here, I'll have someone drive you to a motel," he said.

He expected her to snap at him—*I don't have the money for that*—but she didn't. Instead, she nodded once, not taking her gaze off the front door of the house, and said, "I'd appreciate that."

He looked at that door, too, but didn't see much out of the ordinary. It was open and revealed the darkness inside. The coroner had shown up and he'd lock the place down when he was done until the state police showed up and handled the crime scene investigation. He'd had to request that directly—Hawthorne didn't have the ability to do high-end crime scene investigation, and the state of Nevada didn't have the resources to do it on every single murder in the state, no matter what those damn *CSI* shows led the American public to believe.

But he thought it was necessary here, since he knew in his bones this was a pro, a transient pro, who was probably in California by now.

"I'm sorry, ma'am," he said slowly, "but—"

"You have to ask questions, I know," she said. "You want to know what I saw. I didn't see shit. I got home, I went in, I called his name, and there he was. I didn't even think he was dead for a minute, I'm so damn dumb, and it wasn't for awhile that I realized the stupid shooter could still be in the house. I got outside but I don't remember how, and I don't know how long it took you guys to arrive, and I didn't see anything suspicious except those people—"

She swung a hand back toward the neighbors who had gathered. Didn't matter where a crime happened—Hawthorne, LA—if the coroner arrived, if there was an ambulance, if there was more than one police car, and they stayed for longer than ten minutes, the neighbors came out like vultures to see if someone was really and truly dead.

"Why do you think those people are suspicious?" he asked.

"Because," she said, lowering her voice, "I don't recognize any of them."

He glanced at the crowd—if ten people could be called a crowd. He grabbed his cell from his pocket, tapped on it with his thumb, and bent his head. Without looking at them, he snapped some pictures of them, just to make sure the makeup of the crowd didn't change before he could send someone over there to take names.

"You don't know your neighbors?" he asked as he checked the images.

"When would I get a chance to meet them? I work. Gary's the one who's home all day...."

Her voice trailed off. She glanced at Cahill as if surprised she had said that. She'd surprise herself a lot the next few days, talking as if her husband was still alive.

"Why was he home?" Cahill asked. "I thought he was in the military."

"He was." She sighed. "We thought he was going to get discharged, but lately they'd been talking about redeployment. He had a desk job until a few weeks ago."

"What happened then?" Cahill asked.

Her face colored. "He—nothing."

"Mrs. Storvick," Cahill said, lowering his voice. "I need to know everything, the good and the bad."

"He did too much personal stuff when he should've been working. They called it a leave, but it was a disciplinary action. That's why they were talking about redeploying him. It was a threat."

Cahill nodded, although he hadn't heard of anything like that before. Mostly the guys who ended up here had had too many deployments already. They still had time to serve, so they served it pushing papers, monitoring the weapons, guarding the site. He used to think it was a cush job, and it was for some—but others who came here, guys like Storvick, guys who were one demerit away from dishonorable discharge—for them, the job could be hard.

"How long have you been married, ma'am?" he asked.

She looked at him for the first time. Her eyes were a watery blue and there was more intelligence in them than he expected. He'd never really noticed much past her chest and her attitude back when she waited on him.

She knew he'd asked how long she'd been married because he didn't believe the redeployment bullshit. What he didn't know was if she knew her husband's story was bullshit or if she hadn't suspected it until now.

84

"Two years," she said, her tone flat, without pride.

"And you knew each other how long before you got married?" he asked.

"Ten days," she said.

He raised his eyebrows, still in Andy Griffith mode, not willing to say anything against Storvick, not yet.

"So you didn't know his history," Cahill said.

"Thought I did," she said. "We met in Vegas, and didn't leave each other's side until the ceremony. We talked about everything, I thought."

He noted the two different "thoughts." Her thoughts had clearly changed over the past two years.

"Guess it means something when a guy tells you he's never been married and some counselor tells him he can't commit, but he says he'll commit to you. It means something when he moves from place to place and it's not just because he's military. It means something when he says no one understands him except you." She looked at the front door and shook her head. "It means that the bastard thinks he can reform and he can't and much as he thinks he loves you he doesn't even know what love is."

"I'm sorry," Cahill said, because *when did you realize he wasn't what he seemed?* wasn't the appropriate thing to say at the moment. Although Cahill was going to launch into a variation. "Did he tell you he'd been arrested?"

"Yeah," she said. "In that first ten days, even. He told me. He told me the cops dropped the charges when they realized they had the wrong guy. But they didn't, did they?"

Cahill wasn't going to answer that. Not yet anyway. "What makes you say that?"

"He's so secretive. He was promising money, and there's no way to get money here unless you're doing something illegal or you're a gambler."

"Was he a gambler?" Cahill asked, even though he knew that Storvick wasn't. Cahill knew the compulsive gamblers, too, and Storvick never met with them.

"No," she said. "At least, not at the casino. But he was always talking about big money."

"From the minute you met him?"

She nodded.

"Did he talk to you about it?"

"A little bit." She wiped a hand over her face. "He said he'd handled big money before, and he'd handle it again."

Cahill frowned.

"He said when everything was done, we'd never have to worry. He'd take care of me, he said. Guess that'll never happen." She choked up, swallowed, and actually got control of herself again.

Cahill had seen that sort of thing before. She didn't want to cry for the bastard. The marriage had turned ugly. "Which arrest did he tell you about?"

She turned to him again, that sharp look in her eyes. "There was more than one?" she asked, like he knew she would.

"Five that I've found so far," he said.

"So far? You've managed to look that up since you got here?"

He shook his head. "I've been keeping an eye on your husband, ma'am. I was worried that he might be trouble."

"Because of the arrests?"

"And a few other things," he said, but didn't elaborate. The rumors of the money, the known associates, the trouble at the base, all made Gary Storvick a person of interest any time something happened in Hawthorne.

"What was he arrested for the other times?" she asked. "Was it here?"

"Various places, ma'am," Cahill said. "Wisconsin, the last time."

"All of them for robbery?" She apparently thought the money was stolen. Considering how he lived and how he had talked about it, it probably was.

Cahill kept his voice soft. He wasn't surprised that she didn't know what he'd really been arrested for. What man would tell his wife the truth in this instance? "He was arrested for rape, ma'am."

"Rape?" She raised her voice so loudly that everyone nearby, including the nosy neighbors, looked at her. She noticed it, leaned toward Cahill, and lowered her voice. "You're kidding, right? Rape?"

"Not kidding," he said. "In all five cases, the victim withdrew the charges."

Under duress, the cops thought, but they never had time to pursue. Besides, rape cases were the toughest to prosecute. Prosecutors were always glad to see rape cases go away.

"Rape," she said a third time, and shook her head. "Son of a fucking bitch. So it was a woman that killed him."

Interesting deduction, one he hadn't made. "Not likely," he said. "Rape victims don't usually shoot their attackers years after the assault."

"So maybe it was recent, the asshole," she said.

"You have reason to believe it was?" he asked. That would put a new twist on the case.

"He sure wasn't getting any from me," she said.

Not that that mattered. Many rapists maintained a seemingly healthy sex life with their partners. They got something else out of the rape—dominance, a feeling of power, a sexual rush from inflicting pain.

But Cahill wasn't going to say any of that. She didn't need to think about it at the moment. She was probably on overload anyway.

"Did he do anything else suspicious?" Cahill asked.

"You mean like hanging up the phone when I walked into the room or changing the conversation when I approached his friends? Stuff like that?"

Cahill nodded.

"All the damn time," she said. "I thought he was having an affair."

"Any ideas who with?"

"No," she said. "I just figured—ah, hell. It doesn't matter what I figured, does it? He was a bastard and someone shot him and they probably did me a favor except that I can't go back into my house and oh, God—"

And that was when the tears came. She crumpled against her car, and because he was still playing good cop, he put a hand on her shoulder to comfort her. He caught Brett's eye and waved her over—time to hand the wife off to the real live good cop, and then he sauntered away, heading to the neighbors, still watching like a pack of ghouls.

So the wife hated Storvick. And she'd even expressed a different theory of the crime, one he hadn't considered. Not too likely, but then what was? A hired hit could've come from victims as easily as it came from some underworld figure.

He'd check phone records and activities.

But first he'd talk to the ghouls, and see if they had observed anything the willfully blind wife had missed.

— 22 —

Moira started shaking about ten miles outside of Tonopah. Two killings in one day was one past her quota. Hell, two in one week was one past her quota. And this one she wasn't sure she could justify. She had no idea who the man was, except he knew who she was, and that she'd seen Gary Storvick.

And the man had followed her from Hawthorne.

Which ruled him out as a cop. Right? Because cops didn't change jurisdictions. They had someone else handle it.

Oh, shit. Had she killed a Tonopah cop?

She drove down the stupid highway still in the stupid desert, getting fucking sick of the red rock around her. Ahead, she thought she saw another town, but as they got close she realized they were in a ghost town—ruined and abandoned buildings everywhere, including what was once a fancy brick hotel, certainly the best and biggest hotel she'd ever seen abandoned, taking someone's hopes with it, probably, or the hopes of an entire community—a community now dead.

Like that guy.

She glanced over her shoulder. Kasey was drinking the water, Barbie resting on her lap. She was looking out the window, too, as if she couldn't believe what she saw. She seemed subdued.

"Were those people nice to you?" Moira asked. Really, she was worried if Kasey had seen anything or heard anything, if she'd wandered out and then gone back in, pretending everything was normal when it wasn't.

"Yeah," Kasey said.

"You okay?" Moira asked. If Kasey'd been an adult, she would have added something like, *you seem down* or *what has you upset*?, but she'd learned not to do that with Kasey, because Kasey would then try to be upset just to please Moira.

Damn kid tried too hard to be everything to everyone. Moira wished she knew how to talk to her about that, too. But she didn't. She didn't know how to talk to Kasey and soon it wouldn't be her responsibility at all.

"Fine," Kasey said.

Moira sighed into the silence. She probably wouldn't learn what upset Kasey. Maybe Moira's mood had done it. She usually planned her shoots, maybe not to the detail—how would she know what the layout of Gary Storvick's house was, for example—but at least in the timing of it all. She knew when someone would die and how she would make it happen. She had an exit strategy. She knew what to say if a cop pulled her over.

Only this guy hadn't pulled her over. He had cornered her. That had freaked her out. No one cornered her—

"…that baby?" Kasey was saying.

Shit. She'd been talking and Moira hadn't listened. "What about the baby?"

"She didn't cry," Kasey said.

Moira tilted her head. "Should she have cried?"

"Babies cry," Kasey said.

"Not all the time," Moira said.

Kasey sighed loudly, for effect.

"Why do you think she should've been crying?" Moira asked. "Did someone hurt her?"

"I dunno," Kasey said, but she did. That was the tone she used when she thought she knew the truth and no one would believe her.

"Who hurt her?" Moira asked.

"That man. He was standing right there," Kasey said.

"Did he hit her?" Moira asked.

"You don't hit babies," Kasey said.

"Then why do you think he hurt her?" Moira looked into the rear-view mirror.

"Dunno," Kasey said. She was looking at the Barbie doll.

"You do too," Moira said.

"He had his hand on her."

"On her knee," Moira said.

"She shoulda cried."

"Why?" Moira asked.

Kasey's mouth was a thin line. She clearly wasn't going to say any more. And neither was Moira. Kasey wasn't upset over the shooting. She didn't even know about the shooting. She was upset about something that happened in the store, something that hadn't happened to her, but she had seen, and that made it none of Moira's business because she was never ever going back there.

He couldn't have been a cop because there was no cop car parked nearby. When she drove off, careful to keep her speed reasonable and not peel out of that narrow parking lot, she hadn't seen any other cars at all, except the couple's truck parked to the side of the store.

Not even any cars on the highway. Nothing. The sedan was gone. She'd been checking in her rearview, just in case, and she didn't see him.

But she didn't see the sedan parked nearby either. No cars. The man had just appeared out of nowhere.

Moira put the heel of her hand on her forehead. She was too hot and tired and she was ready for this road to end and this job to be over and the kid to be delivered. Then she'd buy herself the best hotel room in Vegas and she'd take a long cold shower to bring her skin temperature down and she'd buy more aloe (although the stuff she put on after she'd put on some sunscreen and put more on Kasey felt really really good already. It was helping. She didn't have heat stroke or anything, she just had too much sun).

The stress was getting to her, and some of that stress, she knew, was because this trip was damn long and she wasn't alone.

And then she got surprised. He had followed her. That was the only way he knew who she was. And she was justified in shooting him. He'd cornered her and cornering her was wrong.

She glanced in her rearview again. That weird abandoned city was gone, and so was the fancy hotel and there were no cars behind her, no one to observe her, she and Kasey were all alone on this highway, and they were going just fast enough to be travelers, but not too fast, and they had to get to Vegas sometime before this long insane day was over.

Next stop, according to the signs, a place called Beatty. Maybe it was as abandoned as that last town. Maybe she should stop anyway, and get rid of the gun. Because she didn't dare use it again, not even if she got cornered.

Towns like Tonopah didn't have homicide detectives. They used the state police for capital crimes. And maybe Hawthorne did, too. And eventually someone would tie the two shootings together just by the gun, especially if the same agency investigated.

So it was time to get rid of the gun, not just the silencer. She'd be without weaponry for about two hours, maybe more, because she wouldn't have the gun when she dropped off Kasey. She should've patted down that cop (he wasn't a cop, dammit, but he seemed like a cop, that was what was upsetting her. Something in his moves said *cop*) and she should've seen if he had a gun.

Hell, this was Nevada, the West, didn't everyone have guns? Better than the namby pamby Midwest where the gun owners were hunters, for godssakes, and not real hunters like her, but the kind that killed defenseless animals for meat as if there wasn't perfectly good meat in any nearby grocery store.

"Where're we going?" Kasey asked.

Moira looked into the backseat in astonishment. Kasey never asked that question, not in the thousands of miles they'd already traveled.

"Why?" she asked.

"'coz," Kasey said.

"Because why?"

"Because I don't like it here," she said, her voice rising.

Moira smiled. Perfectly stated. She couldn't agree more.

"I don't like it here, either," she said. "I promise. We won't stay anywhere near this stuff. We're going to a big city, and we'll sleep in comfortable beds tonight."

"Good," Kasey said. "And Mickey D's, right?"

"As many Happy Meals as you can eat," Moira promised, knowing she wouldn't have to be the one to make good on it. "I swear."

— 23 —

Analyn watched the ball bounce around the roulette wheel. The people around her cheered and chanted, but she just stared. It was hypnotic, but not all that interesting. She should have tried something else while she tried to kill time.

But she didn't know how to play poker, and she wasn't that fond of blackjack. Craps looked exciting but confusing. Besides, there was only one table open. The number of people on the casino floor was nowhere near capacity. The aisles were designed to handle at least ten across, but mostly couples and friends walked through them now. One or two slot machines had players in rows after rows after rows.

Not even the terminally hopeful seemed to be trying to strike it rich in this economy.

She wasn't striking it rich either. She had planned to lose $500, and as the roulette ball settled on red, she had officially lost $498. She wasn't going to play two more dollars—not that she could, anyway, since she had to bet a minimum of $5 here.

She gathered up her remaining chips, put them back in their plastic carrier, and stood up. No one stopped her. Only the woman running the wheel even noticed her leaving.

Analyn checked her watch as she walked across the casino floor. An hour. The guy next to her had told her he could lose $500 in five minutes. She could have, too, if she had bet it all on one number, like he suggested.

But she wasn't the kind of woman to put all of her money in one place. She felt uncomfortable playing the full $500 at that single roulette wheel. At first, she thought she'd be there forever. The chips kept piling up. She had actually been on a tiny streak. People came over to her, talked to her, sat near her, trying to get her luck to rub off on them.

She hadn't said anything, because if she spoke she would have insulted them. Luck didn't rub off. And it would turn quickly, because luck was never just good. It could also be bad.

During this run, her luck never went bad. It just returned to neutral, and neutral meant the house had a huge advantage. She lost her $500 ($498, actually) bit by bit.

An hour. The guy next her had called that a good run.

If she hadn't been trying to lose the money, she would have called it a fool's errand. Five hundred dollars gone in one hour? That was awful. Five hundred dollars could have paid someone's rent, for heaven's sake.

Then she looked at all the employees trying to blend into the scenery, standing near a post or bent over a blackjack table. Her $500 probably would pay someone's rent—or at least part of it.

She had to remember why she was here. She walked to one of the gilded cages, and made herself take a deep breath. Then she walked to the man behind the counter, and slid the plastic container of chips toward him, just like she'd seen a few other people do.

He counted the chips quickly, dividing them up with a little piece of paper, and speaking each hundred out loud.

"Five thousand," he said without looking at her. Then he pulled open a drawer revealing more cash than she had seen at one time. Did every other teller have that much cash? She glanced around. If so, that was a staggering amount of money.

His hand hovered over the hundreds.

"How do you want it?" he asked.

"Cash," she said.

He finally looked up at her, his expression bland, but behind it she could sense impatience. This man, this skinny little man in his casino uniform, hated his job so much that he could barely contain himself. Or maybe he hated her. Or the customers in the casino. Maybe he just hated.

She forced herself to hold her ground. Men, particularly angry men, frightened her.

"Tens? Twenties? Hundreds?" he asked, his voice edged with contempt.

She cleared her throat so that her voice would be firm. "Hundreds."

He didn't answer. Instead, he counted out the bills, and handed them to her.

She took them, hands shaking. She hadn't even thought to take her wallet out of her purse. She glanced behind her. No one else stood in line.

So she stepped slightly to the side, pulled out her wallet, and clicked the fastener. The bills slid inside just as easily as twenties usually did. For some reason, that surprised her.

Then she glanced at the man a final time. He wasn't watching her. He was putting her chips into other slots, spreading his hands and turning them over, which, she finally realized, was some kind of signal for the cameras above, probably to prove he wasn't pocketing chips.

She grimaced. She couldn't help herself. She didn't like it here, and she wouldn't want to work here.

She was only here because Moira had initially told her to go to a casino and wait.

Go in and out of casinos a lot in the next few weeks, Moira had said after Analyn had hired her. *Make sure you're visible as much as possible. Better to have security cameras on you than friends saying what you did.*

As an alibi, Analyn knew. Moira wanted her to have an ironclad alibi.

Analyn shivered. She didn't want to think about that.

She glanced at her watch. Another fifteen minutes had gone by. Until the meeting time, she would live her life in fifteen minute intervals. She would get some coffee, make sure no one saw her put that $5000 in her wallet (of course someone saw her; people were watching her on the security cameras. But she didn't want some tourist seeing her and following her out of the building, trying to steal the money). Then she would go back to her car, which was parked in that palatial lot at the Venetian, and slowly drive to the meet.

This had to be the longest day of her life.

And it was only going to get longer.

— 24 —

It was hot and there was no shade. Zane stood in the middle of the street with the rest of the neighbors, only he didn't recognize most of them. Some had come over from side streets when they saw the cop cars. A few seemed to materialize from nowhere.

Only the fat lady in her caftan and the elderly couple from down the block looked at all familiar. Zane recognized the old guy from the early mornings, when Zane left the house to get some shut-eye, and the old guy was in his lawn puttering with the flowers. His was the only yard that had actual flowering, non-desert plants. And it was pretty, too.

Zane hovered near the edge of the crowd. He watched the cop cars and the ambulance. None of this was like TV. On TV, everybody parked in an orderly fashion. A few people were clearly in charge and they bantered with each other as they went from room to room. Sometimes they even made dry jokes about the corpse.

No one was joking here. And one cop left the house, bent into the bushes, and barfed. No one barfed on TV except maybe the relatives of the dead person.

Some guy in a lightweight suit was talking to Jenny the wife. Some other guy in a suit had gone in clutching some kind of kit. A few cops stood in the middle of the lawn, yakking about UNLV's chances this year, and another cop was on the driveway talking on the phone, clearly to somebody important. Someone wasn't doing something, but that was all Zane could get from that conversation.

He wished Dirksen hadn't told him to come out here. He felt really exposed. No one was watching him directly, but he wondered if they were watching him sideways and judging him the way he was judging everybody else.

Worse, he didn't have a lot to report. He could've gotten it all from the computer and the cameras he set up. Gary Storvick was dead, the cops were here, and no one knew anything. Whoop-de-do.

Then the cop in the suit who'd been talking to Jenny the wife came walking toward the neighbors. Zane's heart started beating, hard. Crap. He should've gone back inside. He never should've come out here.

He didn't want to talk to a cop. He didn't want to say anything about anything.

"Excuse me," the cop said. "I'm Detective Cahill."

He reached into his pocket and pulled out a wallet thing, opening it briefly so that a bit of metal flashed. Was that a badge? Or did he call it a shield like they did on TV?

He said, "I was wondering if any of you people saw anything unusual today."

They all looked at each other, like they were suddenly friends and needed to consult with each other before answering. Damned if Zane didn't do that, too. He didn't want to be the one to say there'd been this VW van with a mattress tied onto the roof and some woman and a little kid visiting Gary Storvick just before the guy got whacked. Zane didn't want to call any attention to himself at all.

"Well," the fat lady said, pushing her way to the front of the group. Zane got a whiff of perfume, heavy on the musk. "There was this car."

Leave it to her to call the van a car.

"It just peeled out, not a half an hour before Jenny got home."

"Can you describe the car?" the cop asked.

"It was black, some kind of sedan. It had Nevada plates, but I didn't get the number."

Zane was so surprised at the description of the sedan instead of the van that it took him a moment to realize she was describing Davis's car. And Davis did peel out. He was in an awful goddamn hurry because he was afraid he'd lose the van.

"Did you see the driver?" the cop asked.

"Some guy," she said. "He'd been hanging around a lot lately. He'd walk the neighborhood. I thought he was creepy."

So much for keeping a low profile. Davis's stupid idea about parking far away from the house hadn't worked for him. Walking to the house had been dumb, too. Zane would tell him that later, when they got a chance.

If the cops didn't arrest Davis first.

"White? Tall? Dark-haired?" the cop asked.

"White," the fat woman said. "In shape, but not like military, you know. Just not fat."

She said the word "fat" with a bit of regret, like she knew that was how everybody thought of her. That caught Zane's attention and gave him a little more respect for her.

"That guy," the old man said. "I saw him too. He's been here a lot in the last month or two. He visits one of the houses, but I don't think he lives there."

"Why do you say that?" the cop asked.

"Because…" the old man shook his head. "You tell 'em, Evvie. You're the one who noticed."

His wife moved closer to the cop. "He never changed clothes there."

"What do you mean?" the cop asked.

"You come home, you change clothes. You get ready for bed, you take a shower, you leave again, you're usually wearing something different unless you're only home for a few hours. He'd be in that house for eight hours, maybe more, and he'd never change clothes—until he showed up the next day. So he didn't live there. He visited."

The cop was frowning. Zane froze in place. Had the old lady watched him, too? He swallowed hard, compulsively, and the swallow seemed so loud he was afraid the guy next to him could hear it.

"Did he ever talk to Gary Storvick?" the cop asked.

"I don't know," the woman said. "I never saw him talking to anyone."

But she didn't look at Zane and she didn't point him out. Zane wished he could slide out of the conversation, but that would call attention to himself.

"Can you describe him?" the cop asked her.

"Forty-ish, was ex-military, I would guess, just by the way he walked. Athletic. Kept himself in shape. Probably six feet give or take an inch, 190 maybe less, strong chin. Hair could've been brown or dark blond, I couldn't tell."

The cop's eyebrows raised. "That's excellent, ma'am. If we had a sketch artist—"

And he said that like he didn't know if they had a sketch artist.

"—would you be able to work with him?"

"I'd love to," the old woman said.

"She's been observing people up close her whole life," the old guy said with pride. "My Evvie, she likes to watch people."

The cop smiled, as if the comment actually amused him. Then he turned to her. "Did you see anything unusual besides that man?"

"And the sedan peeling out," the old woman said. She looked at the fat woman. "That was an accurate description."

"Thanks," the fat woman said.

"In fact," the old woman said, "unless I miss my guess, that car had a bigger engine than it should have. Like cop cars, you know? They put in faster engines."

"I do know," the cop said, and this time he sounded certain.

Zane swallowed hard again. He tried to will that reaction to go away, but he couldn't seem to stop it. Davis's car had a bigger engine. It was a former cop car, a rebuild, that he had bought cheap. He kept everything in it, just in case he needed stuff.

No one was saying anything. Most everybody was looking at the old woman as if she was a hero or something.

"There was the van," Zane blurted, then wished he hadn't.

The cop looked at him. Zane swallowed again. His cheeks felt hot, not from the sun, but because he was embarrassed. Did most people get embarrassed talking to the cops? He didn't know.

"What van?"

He shrugged, because if he didn't shrug he would've blurted that he had video of the damn van. "It was just some van with a mattress on the top. It was in the driveway for a while."

"What driveway?" The cop's voice was soft, like he was taking pity on Zane for his nervousness. Maybe the cop was. Maybe the cop thought he was some scared teenager, not the hacker hired to monitor Storvick's house.

"Mr. Storvick's," Zane said. "It was there for about a half hour."

"When?"

"Around lunch, maybe? I don't know exactly." He did know exactly, but he couldn't say. And if the cop asked him his name, he'd have to make up something. Because he didn't want to say much more.

"Anyone else see that van?" the cop asked.

Everyone shook their heads, including the nosy old couple.

"But," the old woman said, "if it was at the house over lunch, I wouldn't've seen it. I like to watch the news over lunch and Pa, he sleeps after he has his meal."

"Evvie," the old man said, chastising her fondly.

"You do," she said, and with that, the attention was off Zane.

"Thanks," the cop said. "You've been helpful."

But Zane needed to ask a couple questions, just for Dirksen. Zane couldn't just melt away, not knowing so little.

"Um, sir?" he said. "Is Mr. Storvick all right?"

He figured naïve was the way to go.

The cop gave him a compassionate look. "I'm afraid not, son."

"But the ambulance—"

"Is standard here," the cop said. "We aren't big enough for a coroner's van."

"So he's dead?" Zane asked. "Killed?"

"Yes," the cop said. "And I can't say any more."

He thanked everyone again, then wandered back to the house.

The old lady looked at Zane. "You can always tell they're dead by how the ambulance shows up," she said.

He looked at her. She had bright blue eyes, and flushed cheeks.

"What do you mean?" he asked, because he couldn't leave her statement hanging. He would wonder about it for a long time if he didn't ask.

"If the sirens are off when it arrives, then you know it's been called for a person who's already dead. If it comes with sirens blaring, someone thinks the person is still alive. If it comes sirens blaring and leaves with the sirens off, the person's dead."

Zane stared at her. She was enjoying this, he realized, and the thought freaked him out in a really icky way.

"Told you," the old man said. "My Evvie watches everything."

Zane's heart rate had increased again. It felt like his heart was trying to beat its way out of his chest.

"How come I've never met your parents?" the old woman asked.

There it was. The question he'd been waiting for, in veiled form. *Who are you?* she was asking.

"It's just my dad," he said, electing Lyman in his mind to play that role. "He works third shift."

And he did, third shift surveillance, watching Gary Storvick, not that he'd have to do that any more.

"He doesn't like to introduce himself because we move a lot," Zane added.

Several people in the crowd nodded. That explanation was never a problem in military towns.

"You tell him to keep the doors locked," the old woman said. "We don't know what happened here, but that guy looked scary. I've been telling Pa that. I thought we should call the cops, but Pa said you can't call the cops just because you don't like the look of someone."

"You can't," the old man said.

Good thing they didn't or they would have blown the entire surveillance. Zane would have to tell Dirksen just how bad Davis had been.

Jeez, and Davis thought he was God's gift to surveillance. Asshole.

"How long do you think they'll be here?" Zane asked the old couple, nodding at the cops.

"Until something else important happens, I suppose," the old man said.

Zane looked at the old lady. She seemed like the only one who knew what was going on. But she shrugged, too.

He didn't want to be outside any longer, but he didn't want to call attention to himself any more than he already had.

So he didn't move, and he watched the house. Just like he was paid to do.

— 25 —

In the light of the afternoon sun, Beatty didn't look real. Moira pulled off the highway into a faux adobe truck stop. Everything looked cleaner here: the parking lot, the buildings, the streets themselves. Bright, with the sunlight so white that it was almost blinding.

The heat didn't seem worse here, though. Or maybe she had just gotten used to it.

Her bottle of water was long gone. So was Kasey's. Moira got out of the van, then opened the back and helped Kasey get out. They went inside, hand-in-hand.

It was cooler in the truck stop, but not frigidly cold. The front doors were open, which was weird because the air conditioner was on. The store seemed to go on forever. It had clothes and CDs and snacks and candy in bins. A restaurant sat in the corner, but it wasn't a real restaurant. It was a fast food chain—not McDonald's, fortunately, or Kasey would have said something.

They walked down the hall to the ladies' room, past showers and phone banks. The bathrooms were the size of the truck stop in Hawthorne. Moira got done first and she put cold water on her face. Sunburned, but not badly enough to blister. Still, spending the next few days in 60-degree air conditioning sounded like heaven at the moment.

Too bad most places kept their AC at 75 these days.

She put on more aloe, then followed it with sunscreen. When Kasey came out, she did the same. Kasey tilted her face upwards, letting Moira slather her skin. Moira rubbed the lotion in, all the time thinking about the gun in her purse.

She didn't know how she was going to get rid of it here. The town was too clean. Everything seemed like it had been outlined in sharp relief.

Besides, she needed that gun. What if someone else followed her?

She bought more water, some Gatorade, and two donuts that looked reasonably fresh. Something to tide them over for the final push to Vegas.

Then she went outside and stood for just a minute. A few cars, dust-covered, looked like they'd been parked for a while. Two semis. One Fed Ex truck—not a delivery truck, but one of the ground trucks that brought packages from one town to the next.

And that was it. Nothing she recognized. Not the Lexus with the woman from Hawthorne, not the sedan. Moira was pretty sure the guy she killed had been in that sedan because she hadn't seen it since just outside Tonopah.

But she couldn't be certain, and it was the lack of certainty that was getting to her.

If she was alone, she would have taken 58 into Death Valley. Beatty called itself the Gateway to Death Valley, like that was something to be proud of. But she was the Gateway to Death Valley. Then she smiled at the thought.

At least, she'd been the Gateway to Death Valley for Gary Storvick and that guy in the sedan. And Kasey's father and those guys in Salt Lake and Lincoln and Des Moines and a few others along the way. Guys she didn't want to think about anymore.

She shook off the thought. Looked at the garbage can nearby, thought about dumping her gun. No one was looking.

But Nevada liked cameras, and she had no idea how many were in Beatty or where they were. Better to keep the gun and not get caught than dump the gun and lead someone right to her.

Although she could go back to the ladies' room and put the gun in the donut bag, then dump the bag.

Then she'd do the meet without the gun. And that wouldn't feel right.

She usually wasn't a gambler, but she could bet on not getting caught between here and Vegas. No one was following her, she knew that much. And she'd see a cop approaching on 95. Once she was in Vegas, she was safe.

She'd just follow the plan.

She'd deviated from the plan in Tonopah and it had cost her. She'd had to shoot someone unexpectedly.

She wasn't going to deviate any more.

She was going to drive to Vegas, meet Analyn, finish the job, and then sleep for three days.

With her gun.

Dammit.

— 26 —

Finally the crowd started to disburse. First a guy in a baseball cap wandered off, hands in his pockets. Then another old guy. And another.

They were all starting to realize what Zane already knew. Watching people was a whole lotta nothing interspersed with moments of action. If you stopped watching the nothing, you missed the action.

But the cops had settled into a rhythm, talking to each other, joking, watching the house. The body came out in a bag on a gurney, followed by the coroner. Jenny the waitress watched but didn't run over there. She didn't try to wrap her arms around the corpse and sob like people did on TV, like Zane'd actually seen his Aunt Sadie do when his Uncle Thomas had died.

Jenny the waitress didn't move at all, not until that cop—Cahill—pulled her aside and handed her over to some chick cop, who put an arm around her and led her to a car. They gestured at the house itself—probably asking if she wanted stuff—and Jenny the waitress shook her head *no*. Then she got into the car with the chick cop and they drove away.

It was ending. That was why the guy in the baseball cap left, why the other guy had followed. If Zane guessed correctly, the old lady, her husband, and the fat lady would be the last to leave.

He didn't want to be anymore a part of that group than he already was. So he eased out of the crowd too, waiting until no one looked in that direction before slinking back to the house and going in through the garage.

It was blessedly cool out of the sun. He hadn't realized how hot he had gotten. He went inside through the kitchen door, grabbed one of Davis's Gatorades—let the asshole complain—and sucked it down even though the stuff tasted like sweetened piss. When he finished, he wiped his mouth, grabbed a Red Bull, and pulled out his cell.

His hands were shaking, not from the heat or from released tension, but because he had to call Dirksen again.

Goddamn Davis for leaving him alone with this.

Zane hit Dirksen's number on the cell. Dirksen picked up midway through the first ring.

"He's dead," Zane said.

"Figured as much when you told me about the blood," Dirksen said. "How'd you guys miss a murder?"

"I wasn't here," Zane said.

"How do you know?" Dirksen said.

"No one went in the back," Zane said. "We have cameras there."

"So Davis missed it." Dirksen sounded odd, distant, like he wasn't even really talking to Zane. Musing, maybe. "You think it was the girl?"

"Girl?" Zane asked.

"The woman in the van. The one with the kid. You think it was her?"

"I don't know," Zane said. "I can go back through the video, look to see if anyone else arrived."

"I already did," Dirksen said. "You sent me enough. We know that Gary was alive when she arrived and we didn't see him when she left. If she's the contact, she's good. And he didn't supply anything."

"But if she's not the contact?"

"Then maybe the wife killed him. How the hell should I know?" Dirksen said. "What'd the cops say?"

"They interviewed the wife, but I don't think they think she did it. They were asking us what we saw."

"Us? Lyman back? Davis around?"

"No, sir." Zane moved into the living room. Another cop car had left. So had the ambulance. "I meant the crowd. I was hanging out with the locals like you told me."

"Tell me what the cops asked," Dirksen said.

So Zane did.

Dirksen was silent during Zane's recap. Then he said, "You know anyone working the scene?"

"I don't know cops," Zane said, letting the full horror of the idea into his voice.

"You recognize any of them?"

"The guy who talked to us said his name was Cahill."

"*Doug* Cahill?"

"I don't know," Zane said. "Detective Cahill, that's all I know."

"He's in charge of the investigation?"

"Yes, sir. You want me to talk to him some more?"

"I want you to keep an eye on that house. See if anyone else turns up. If the meet didn't go down, then Storvick's contacts are going to want to get inside. They'll search. I want to know who they are and when they get there and what they leave with. You got that?"

"Yes, sir."

"You hear from Lyman or Davis?"

"No, sir."

"Then you work the scene until they get back. It's on you, kid. You got that?"

"Yes, sir," he said, but he was speaking to air. Dirksen had cut the connection.

Zane set the phone down before launching into a series of curses that did not make him feel better. He was the junior man on the team. He wasn't supposed to run everything. Bastards had left him alone with this and they'd pay for that.

He sat down in front of the computer, backed up the current footage, and looked to see if he had missed anything. He even zoomed in on the open front door, but only got shadows.

110

Nada. Zip. Zilch.

He picked up the phone and called Lyman. "I need you, man," he said when Lyman picked up. "Everything's gone to hell."

And strangely, Lyman didn't even ask him what he meant.

— 27 —

Cahill walked the house one more time. Someone had aspirations to *House Beautiful*, and it wasn't Gary Storvick. The wife had put all her energy into this place, probably because she couldn't put her energy into Storvick and they didn't have kids.

She probably didn't know yet—maybe she would never know—that the lack of kids was almost as big a blessing as Storvick's death.

The state crime scene guys were still working the kitchen. Cahill had told them that this looked like a pro job to him, which meant the evidentiary record had to be stellar. No slips, no misses, nothing overlooked.

Which was why he was walking through the house. He wanted to let them know which rooms needed dusting, which rooms needed investigating besides that kitchen.

His first destination had been the master bedroom—if, indeed, the bedroom with the slightly larger square footage in a 1950s ranch was a "master" bedroom.

The bed had been made with military precision, although it was hard to tell, what with all the ruffles and pillows and dust catchers. Again, not a man's bedroom, and certainly not a bedroom any man would take a lover into. The wife would notice immediately if one of those decorative pillows was out of place.

But nothing seemed out of place. The second bedroom with its smaller bed and lovely quilt was clearly a guest room and still had vacuum marks on the carpet.

The bathroom smelled perfumy, and had more decorations than the bedroom. The only thing out of place was a few blond hairs that didn't look like they belonged to Storvick or the wife. They could have belonged to anyone, but he would have the crime scene techs go over the bathroom, just in case.

He went back to the living room, careful to avoid those drying footprints, and let himself outside.

The crowd was gone, the cars were gone except for the crime scene van and his car, and the ambulance was gone, taking the body with it.

This one had him worried. Given Storvick's past, given his dealings, anyone could've killed him. Cahill supposed he shouldn't rule out the wife, but he had a hunch her alibi and the time of death would do that for him. If she had killed Storvick, she was one cool customer, and one great actress, her talents wasted in this one-horse town.

He had almost reached his car when his cell rang.

He glanced at the face. The number had been blocked. He hadn't seen that since he'd left LA.

If this had been LA, he'd've let this go to voice mail. By the end, too many people had his personal cell, and all kinds of unsavory types called him, blocking the number so he couldn't see it when he answered.

The numbnuts didn't realize that he would get the number along with the bill. If he didn't want to wait that long, he'd make a phone call to the cell phone company and ask. It was his phone, after all. He didn't need the court to get his own damn records.

So he'd moved to Nevada and gotten a new phone, courtesy of the department here. He'd let the old number—and its old associations—go slack.

So this blocked number had him intrigued.

As he answered, he didn't say hello. He didn't give his name. He just said, "What?"

"Douglas Cahill, the great detective." Sarcasm and a familiar voice. An LA voice. Cahill shivered despite himself. Someone had tracked him down. He couldn't quite put a name to the voice, but he would have to. Because this was not how good guys approached him.

He hung up. His heart was pounding rapidly. He made himself take deep breaths to calm down.

The phone rang. He looked at it.

The blocked number again.

To answer? Not to answer? Now *that* was the question, screw Shakespeare. Shakespeare had never had to deal with voice mail.

Cahill answered. "What?"

"You don't know who I am, do you?" The voice sounded amused. "You still owe me, Douglas Cahill, the world's greatest detective."

The hair rose on the back of Cahill's neck and he actually looked around, trying to see if anyone was in the position to overhear this call.

So far as he could tell, he was alone on the street.

"I don't give out this number," he said, which was somewhat true. He'd made a new policy when he'd moved from LA. He didn't give his personal cell to scumbags.

"Then you should ask yourself who has the resources to get it on his own."

"Anyone with brains enough to call the Hawthorne Police switchboard," Cahill snapped. "So stop playing games. I'm busy."

"Ah, Doug. So soon we forget. It's Dirksen."

Shit. Dirksen. Of all the scumbags to track him down, it would be the one he really and truly did owe a favor to.

"What do you want?"

"I understand you're handing the Gary Storvick case," Dirksen said.

Cahill went cold. Dirksen was big in the Southwest. He did business everywhere from Dallas to Los Angeles. He liked Vegas. He liked money. He spent a lot of it and he made a lot more. He had his fingers in damn near everything.

But Cahill had thought he had gone far enough north to get away from Dirksen's interests. There wasn't enough money in Hawthorne to attract his attention. Not from the casino, not from the Depot, not from anywhere.

Yet somehow Dirksen had fingers here. How many people knew that Cahill was on this case? The dispatch. The chief. The state police.

Of course. Dirksen had someone in the state police.

"Yeah, I caught the case," Cahill said. "So?"

"So I need some information," Dirksen said.

"Then read the paper like everyone else," Cahill said and hung up.

He was shaking now. He got into his car, started it, cranked the AC, and the phone rang again. He stared at it. Fucking Dirksen. He thought he'd left Dirksen behind with the other crap he'd put up with in LA.

But the man had his number, literally, and that wasn't good. Cahill picked up the phone.

"You're a bit behind the times," Dirksen said. "No one reads the papers any more."

Cahill didn't say anything. He made sure the windows were rolled up.

"They use the Internet," Dirksen said. "You know the nice thing about connectivity? It's miraculous. I'm hundreds of miles away from you, and I know exactly where you are. Your phone has a GPS. I am looking at your location right now. It'll take a few clicks of my mouse, but I'll be able to know where you are, when you are, what you are. I'll be able to find out everything you've been doing since you left Los Angeles, because you didn't cover your tracks. You bought a house—a nice big house, in a town that doesn't specialize in big houses. Paid 200K, which has to be the top of the market in that hellhole. Then you—"

"What do you want?" Cahill asked.

"Everything you have on Storvick."

"I don't have much. He croaked just a few hours ago."

"How?"

Cahill suppressed a sigh. "Two shots. A pro. One of yours?"

"No," Dirksen said, and that was when Cahill caught a clue. Dirksen was worried. Something hadn't gone according to plan.

The shakes left. If Dirksen was worried, he was vulnerable. If he was vulnerable, he needed Cahill more than Cahill needed him.

After all, Dirksen had old dirt on Cahill, stuff that could've taken his job in LA, but no one would care about here. He'd been honest when he came on board.

I did some stuff in LA that wasn't quite on the up-and-up, he'd said to the chief in the interview here. *You stay there long enough, you meet the wrong people, you bargain with them, you lose. I'm tired of losing.*

The chief had looked at him, then smiled. The smile had been slow. *I worked Vegas in the 70s. It's quieter here.*

Except when contract killers came to town and killed off the local lowlife.

"I help you on this," Cahill said, "and it's the last time. We're done. You got that?"

"I usually don't have need of small town cops in Butt Fuck Nevada," Dirksen said, which was another clue. The man didn't have anyone here. Someone else had contacted him. Maybe not the state police at all.

"But you have need today," Cahill said. "Why?"

"That's none of your concern," Dirksen said, which made it Cahill's concern. The man didn't play for small amounts of money. He was big time, very big time, and he usually didn't fuck with lowlifes like Storvick.

"Storvick working with you?" Cahill asked.

"No." Dirksen said.

Cahill leaned back in the seat. Despite the air conditioning, his shirt was sticking to the upholstery.

"Steal something from you?"

"No," Dirksen said.

"Had information for you?"

Dirksen hesitated. Just a microsecond, but enough to give himself away. "No."

"Then what's the interest?" Cahill asked.

"Didn't expect him to die today," Dirksen said. "Who killed him?"

"I don't know yet," Cahill said. "You got any ideas?"

"Follow the money," Dirksen said.

"What money?" Cahill asked.

But Dirksen didn't answer that either. The man was smart. If he wasn't smart, he wouldn't have survived as long as he had.

"If I find out who killed Storvick," Cahill said, "and I tell you, what're you going to do?"

"Depends," Dirksen said.

"Kill him?" Cahill asked.

"Silly question, Detective. I don't kill people."

"No," Cahill said. "You hire it out. Only someone beat you to this guy."

"I would not have killed Gary Storvick."

"Because he was valuable? A serial rapist always looking to make a buck?"

"I don't really care about his relationship with women," Dirksen said. That sentence was deliberate. Dirksen didn't care about Storvick's documented criminal activities. But he did care about the money.

"What could this guy have that would interest you so much?" Cahill asked.

"What do you have that interests me?" Dirksen asked.

"A badge," Cahill said quietly.

"Hell, no," Dirksen said. "The badge is incidental. You have knowledge, my old friend. That's all. Just some knowledge. Which I hope you'll share."

"I don't know who killed him," Cahill said.

"That may not be the most important piece of information that you're currently missing," Dirksen said. "But you are already behind. Don't you know that murders usually get solved in the first forty-eight hours?"

"You watch too much television," Cahill said.

"I don't watch television," Dirksen said. "Except, of course, the financial news. Which is dismal."

"Even for you?" Cahill asked.

"It depends on what you find. Keep in touch, old friend," Dirksen said and hung up.

Cahill clutched the phone in his right hand, then closed his eyes. How could he have forgotten Dirksen? The "old friend" when things were going well, "detective" when things were going badly.

Cahill wasn't afraid of many people, but Dirksen was one. The man had contacts. He'd killed at least two dirty cops that Cahill had known about—not that he was sorry to see them go. Fortunately, he hadn't caught those cases. He liked to think he was ethical enough to put Dirksen's men away. He had told the investigating detective that the cops had ties to Dirksen.

That piece of information had been shitcanned. Apparently they weren't the only ones with ties to Dirksen.

Hell, maybe that was the reason for the initial "detective" from Dirksen. Someone had told him that Cahill had tried to get him investigated for those killings.

He sighed. It didn't matter. If Dirksen had wanted him dead for that, he would've died before he left LA.

Right now, he had to figure out what interested Dirksen and how it tied into the murder.

Now he had two reasons to investigate—it was his job, and it might be his life.

— 28 —

Las Vegas actually loomed on the horizon.

It wasn't fully dark yet, but the city's lights were so bright, so colorful, that they changed the sky from a powerful blue to a hazy yellowish glow. At first, Moira thought she was looking at part of the Air Force base, but she wasn't. She was staring at the city.

And she was relieved.

Relieved, even though they had to go to the far side of town. South and east. The Boulder Highway. And here she was coming in from the north and west, at least forty-five minutes away. She had to make sure she didn't drive too fast, call attention to herself once she was here.

She looked in her rearview at Kasey. Kasey who was staring at the outside as if it were something alien.

"You okay, kiddo?" Moira asked.

Kasey nodded. She knew Vegas was their destination. Moira had actually told her a day or so ago.

Moira couldn't quite tell the kid's mood. She couldn't tell if Kasey was happy or worried. She hadn't been able to read Kasey all that well this entire trip. Kids were supposed to be open books, but that was probably as much of a fairy tale as the fact that your parents were supposed to love you.

The only time Moira had seen Kasey show an emotion was when Moira broke into Kasey's dad's house. The bastard had double locks that

Moira had to pick and a security system she had to shut down. He'd kept Kasey in the basement, of course. Besides being a cliché, Midwestern basements were mostly soundproof by virtue of being made of concrete and underground.

He'd been in the room with Kasey, little Kasey, little half-naked Kasey, surrounded by dolls and stuffed animals and a webcam and images that even now Moira didn't like thinking about.

He'd turned on Moira and he had a gun beside his digital camera, the one he was using for still photos. He'd pointed it at her, and she had to shoot him right then and there, and Kasey had screamed, and Moira had to calm her down, and that took some work.

She'd had to deal with Kasey and that room. First Moira made sure he was inside. Then she cleaned up the computer and closed that room up tight. No one would find him for days, maybe weeks, thanks to his own stupid planning.

Somehow Moira got Kasey cleaned up and dressed in real little-kid clothes, not that porn crap he wanted her to wear, and then she let Kasey pick out which things she wanted to take with her. Kasey hadn't wanted anything from that room. She wouldn't even go back in there.

She wanted all of the boxes now in the back of the van, boxes that he had never unpacked, the bastard, just left sitting outside that room to taunt her. Stuff he'd thrown into boxes the day he had taken Kasey from her mom and squirreled her five states away.

Kasey had reached inside the top box and taken out the Barbie, and she had hardly let the doll out of her clutches ever since. She even slept with the blasted thing.

Moira hadn't apologized for the shooting or the blood or the fact that some of the spray had hit Kasey in the face. Moira figured an apology would put them on the wrong footing, that Kasey wouldn't respect her.

Moira had no idea if Kasey respected her. But she respected Kasey. That kid had held up through thousands of miles and heat and lots of instruction, instruction she'd followed without questioning.

Kasey was clutching that Barbie now, bouncing it, and not saying anything.

The kid had been useful. Just like the mattress on the roof, and the boxes, and the nearly broken-down van. People made assumptions. A down-on-her-luck mom, moving, with her pretty daughter, going somewhere new, trying again.

It helped that they were both slight and both blond. It helped that they had the same thousand-yard stare. No one asked, assuming some asshole had put them through the ringer.

Assholes had put them through the ringer, but different assholes at different times.

"You ready to get to Vegas?" Moira asked.

"Dunno," Kasey said.

Moira had never asked how long the kid had been with her dad. She didn't know a lot about it, just the facts, ma'am. Hell, the asshole's website had been fact enough. She would've taken him out just from the look of that site, but she wouldn't have shot him so quickly if it weren't for Kasey. Moira would have made it last a little longer, gotten the names of all of his partners and compatriots, found a few more assholes to get rid of.

She hadn't had that luxury with Kasey there. Instead, Moira only grabbed the obvious files. The kid had been traumatized enough.

"You remember your mom?" Moira asked.

Kasey didn't move. The Barbie kept bouncing. She pretended she didn't hear.

Moira wasn't sure how to take that. Yes? No? Unwilling to talk? Probably unwilling to talk. Too much had happened to Kasey. She wasn't going to be vulnerable with anyone, not even Moira, who had saved her.

"We'll see her soon," Moira said. "You think about what you want to tell her."

Kasey kept bouncing the damn doll. And didn't say anything.

But what was there to say, really? To a kid like Kasey, nothing was true until it happened. The rest was empty promises.

Moira wanted to tell her that she understood. She wanted to talk about the system and how to avoid it. She wanted to thank Kasey for being such a help.

But she didn't say anything, either.

She just drove, watching Vegas reveal itself in the distance, like a stripper coming out of a cake, one glittering piece at a time.

— 29 —

The hotel on the old Boulder Highway wasn't as crummy as Analyn expected. Her SUV, two years old but shiny, big, and expensive, wasn't out of place here. The other cars in the lot were big and relatively new, too, just not brand new.

The hotel was three stories and rambling, big for its day, which was probably fifty years ago. It called itself a hotel, but she would've called it a motel.

The neighborhood around it was built-up but seedy, although not Vegas-seedy. Vegas-seedy terrified her, made her clutch her purse to her chest, made her walk a little too fast. Vegas-seedy included drug deals on the street, hookers with glazed eyes, broken bottles in the gutter.

This place had the required pawn shops (but Vegas specialized in pawn shops), the barred windows (but the farther you went from the strip, the more barred the windows became), and the ancient bar that probably had ancient barflies inside. It wasn't so much scary as it was old. Once upon a time, this neighborhood had been The Place To Gamble.

Now it was forgotten in the megalopolis on the Strip, places that catered to tourists, not the working stiffs who had built the Boulder Dam.

There was a parking spot near the hotel's front door. She parked, got out, and felt a flutter in her stomach. She hadn't eaten because she expected to be queasy. Being nervous always made her queasy.

But she wasn't so much queasy as excited.

She was going to see Kasey again.

She hadn't seen the pictures. The detective on the case had told her about them. He'd cropped one, showed her the face, and confirmed what he already knew: that this was her daughter.

Then he told her how hard it would be for the police to track her ex down. They would have to contact the police in the town he was in, and there was no guarantee they had the right town. They also contacted the FBI, but the FBI these days didn't care about kiddie porn. They cared about terrorists.

The detective hadn't sounded encouraging.

Then he'd slid her a piece of paper. *Sometimes these people can help*, he said. *They're not cheap.*

They weren't cheap. And they sent her to other people who weren't cheap. And finally she got Moira on the phone, Moira with her dull flat voice, Moira who said, *If she's alive, I'll bring her to you, and you won't have to worry about that asshole again.*

Analyn liked the "if she's alive." Not because of the sentiment—the sentiment had terrified her—but because Moira was the only one to acknowledge Analyn's greatest fear, that her daughter was already dead.

Analyn had checked with the detective, who said he had no news, and repeated it twice more as Analyn tried to vet Moira through him.

So she took that as permission, and she'd hired Moira, and she was afraid she'd regret it, only first thing, Moira had sent her a digital photo of her daughter clutching her favorite Barbie and sitting on a car seat, boxes of possessions behind her. Analyn had recognized the teddy bear sticking out of one as the bear she had given her daughter at their last Christmas.

She got a photo every couple of days. A different photo, showing her daughter with a different background in different clothes, in that same car seat, clutching that same doll.

Analyn knew it was real. She wasn't going to give money until she had her daughter. Money for child, which was okay. She could handle that, so long as she had Kasey.

Analyn wanted to fly to Moira, and Moira said no. She didn't want the cops to think that she was connected to Kasey's disappearance in any way. Analyn understood that. So then, she wanted Moira and Kasey to fly to her, and Moira said no. The thing that prevented the FBI from working on her daughter's case prevented Moira and Kasey from flying. Too many rules, too many regulations, too many mandates. Proof of identity, destination, cameras everywhere.

And Moira didn't like cameras, except as a way to keep track of Kasey.

Analyn got out of her car and walked inside. She took a room, just like Moira had told her to, first floor, toward the back. The guy at the counter didn't even think the request strange. He just told Analyn where to park her car. Then he handed her a key—an old-fashioned key on a plastic chain with a number engraved on it, a system the hotel had probably used since it was founded, and then he went back to his paperwork.

She left, moved the SUV, and let herself into the room. It smelled of disinfectant. The air conditioner was on low, but the room was cool enough. The TV was new, flat-screen HD, and attached to the wall. That was the only non-1950s part of the room.

She sat on the edge of the bed and looked at her watch.

An hour. Just an hour.

And then she and Kasey could go home.

— 30 —

Bastiano Dirksen owned a penthouse suite at the Wynn—or he liked to think he did. He certainly paid enough for the place, and the hotel/casino looked the other way whenever he added personal items.

And the suite was filled with personal items. Most of the hotel's furniture was gone, except in the living room, where he entertained guests. He had turned the second bedroom into an office, taking his hand-carved mahogany desk out of storage and placing it near the wall, the credenza, with its computer table, facing away from the window—from any reflections, for that matter, from glass or mirrors or even well polished silver. He let no one in that room, not even his own people. And he spent most of his time in it.

He was there now, using one of fifteen cell phones that he owned. The hotel phone sat on the only piece of hotel furniture that was still in the room—a long dresser that (fortunately) matched the desk. Everything else, from the framed art to the sculptures, belong to him.

He had even installed a coded lock on the door, which the hotel had complained about until he reminded them that he had removed everything of theirs and didn't they recall that the customer was always right?

The manager he had spoken to looked like he had swallowed an entire grove of lemons, but he had allowed the lock. The compromise was that the rest of the suite had to be cleaned daily by a hotel maid. Which meant that one of Dirksen's people had to sweep the place for bugs and cameras every day, but he considered it a small price to play for such a free room in such a marvelous location.

He had originally planned to stay a mere six months while his high-end condo got completed. He could see the condo from his bedroom window—or what there was of the condo, which was steel girders and a crane that hadn't moved in nearly a year.

He'd been in his suite for nearly two years, and that suite cost significantly more than he ever would have paid had the condo been finished. But of course, it wasn't.

Vegas got hit harder than any other major city in the West on the housing meltdown—and the moment the good times stopped, so did the building. No amount of cajoling got his deposit back. The developer swore that he would finish the condos soon.

So Dirksen, with some help from a few friends, convinced the developer to pay for Dirksen's suite until the building started again. The developer found the funds each and every month, but Dirksen's friends—who just happened to be in his employ—had mentioned that they doubted the developer would be able to pay much longer.

Or—correction—pay cash. They doubted he would be able to pay cash. He would, of course, continue to pay in whatever way Dirksen thought equitable until the building resumed on the bank of condos out the window.

Dirksen was forty-seven and would have been heavyset if it weren't for the three hours of exercise he performed daily. Cardio, strength training, some boxing. He was still a large man—a former defensive end with a pro career shortened by one bad injury and several citations for illegal betting. It had been his own fault that he got caught. He was, after all, betting on his own games, and he was young and stupid, unsure how the world worked.

But after that, he learned, and he learned well.

He still could get taken, though—sometimes by surprises like the economic meltdown, which he had once believed wouldn't touch him since real estate was the one investment he didn't dabble in, and sometimes by his own hopeful nature, which he was beginning to believe happened in this case.

He had been staking out Gary Storvick for nearly a month, based on some very good intel from a variety of sources. Dirksen had heard for years about the missing cash sent to Iraq. He'd even traced some of it, which ended up in the pockets of arms dealers and private contractors and some Very Bad People, people on the Terrorist Watch List.

Dirksen wasn't a smart man, but he was a savvy man, and he knew about cash. Cash couldn't be traced. People thought they could keep track of it, but they couldn't. He wasn't the only person who knew that about cash, and he had been willing to bet some of his own hard-earned money that some of that cash got siphoned off at every single stop along the way to Iraq and inside Iraq itself.

So he spent years looking for people who had cash to sell.

Which sounded silly—in fact, back in his pro ball days, he would have thought it silly. But American dollars had a value, a value that some people—particularly people from overseas—were willing to pay a premium for. They weren't hurting for money per se, but they were hurting for cash.

At last he heard about $15 million, squirreled in a warehouse near one of the West Coast shipping ports. The cash had been taken off the top of each shipment heading to Iraq, and stored here until it was no longer hot.

Had the sellers been pros, not amateurs, they would have known that the cash was never hot. It was unmarked. Once it crept its way into the money supply, it would vanish.

But amateurs expected to get caught, so they acted guilty. And they lost money on their little theft by storing the cash in that warehouse, instead of moving the cash into the money supply. If they were really worried about it, they could've laundered it.

But they hadn't done any of that.

They had sat on it, and paid the rent on the warehouse.

He just had to know where that warehouse was.

So close. So damn close. And then Gary Storvick had to get himself murdered, probably by his informant.

Who now knew where the money was—and Dirksen didn't. He had the amount of money—$15 million. He had the number of the warehouse itself, thanks to the hacking the kid had done in Hawthorne. Storvick had given the caller the warehouse number, and promised more in person.

The exact location, given today.

Supposedly.

All those years of investigation, one month of stakeout—and salaries to his incompetent employees—and he now had nothing to show for it.

Except some video of a little blond woman, a child, and of Gary Storvick's last known appearance. And a bit of a lucky break, if he could call it that, with The World's Greatest Detective, good old Doug Cahill, on the case.

Cahill, who could be bought.

Cahill, who was afraid of him.

Cahill, who tried to sound brave and strong and tough on the phone, but who would cooperate anyway.

Dirksen sighed. He'd been tracing that van's license plate (Wisconsin, of all places!) and actually getting blocked by his own software. He had alerts coming up, warning him of police traces connected to that van and those plates.

He had to figure out a way around that.

Or maybe he would just call good old Doug Cahill and have him use police software to find the woman.

After all, Cahill was in his pocket—if he only used him properly.

— 31 —

Red and blue lights, swirling through the interior of her van. Moira glanced in her rearview, saw Kasey half-turned toward the back, saw a Las Vegas Police Department car tailing her too close on the Boulder Highway.

She cursed under her breath. Five minutes from her destination. Five stinking minutes.

She thought of flooring it, but this ancient van with its rusted underbelly wouldn't outrun a cop car, not for five miles, probably not for five feet. She couldn't accelerate fast enough to get away from him.

The last thing she wanted to do was shoot him in front of Kasey, but she might have no choice.

Moira pushed some hair away from her face, looking for a parking lot with easy entrance (and exit), and said as she pulled into it, "Stay quiet, honey. Let me talk to the policeman."

As if Kasey would say anything. She'd been abnormally quiet since Moira had mentioned her mother, not that Kasey had ever been a chatterbox.

Moira stopped the van and rolled down the window. Her hand was shaking as she got her license and the proof of insurance out of the glove box. Her heart was pounding.

Had they found the Hawthorne guy in Tonopah? *Was* he a cop, then? He'd looked like a cop. Undercover, maybe, but he had a cop walk. Damn him.

The cop swaggered over—female, dammit, which made things worse. No flirting, no batting eyelashes. Nothing except…

Moira gave Kasey one last glance, winked, and nodded once. Moira would go for barely-holding-it-together brave.

The cop said in a monotone, "License and registration, please."

Moira handed over her license, the one she'd been using since Montana, anyway, and the insurance card. Then asked, in her best panicked-but-hiding-it voice, "Can I ask what this is about, Officer?"

Polite, but scared.

The cop looked at the license. "Asked for registration too."

Moira bit a shaky lower lip. "It—the—I—this is my boyfriend's van. He loaned it to me to get here. I've got a job at the Mirage, my old boss hired me back, but I couldn't get here with my stuff, so he loaned us the van, and he's flying in this weekend to get it and drive it back, you can call him if you want…."

The cop stared at her. Hard brown eyes, tanned skin, a mouth already starting to turn down. Assessed, looked at the license. Then leaned in.

"How old's your daughter?"

God, Moira didn't know. She hadn't asked, she didn't know how to lie about that. What if she answered wrong—the kind of wrong that would be obvious to anyone who knew children? She didn't care about ages, just results and she was five fucking miles away from having them, thank you very goddamn much you fucking pig.

She made herself breathe, and as she did, Kasey said, "I'm going to be seven on May 16!"

God bless the child, she used her chipper "bye-bye voice."

"You upset about moving to Las Vegas?" the cop asked Kasey.

"I was borned here," Kasey said, making a grammatical error. Moira almost—almost—looked at her in surprise. The one thing Kasey never did was make grammatical mistakes. As if someone had beaten the English language into her one declension at a time.

"I was, too," the cop said. "Where were you born?"

"Lake Mead Hospital."

Good God, the child was telling the truth. Moira wanted to applaud her.

The cop looked at Moira. "Wisconsin to Las Vegas is a long way to go in a borrowed van."

"Yes, ma'am," Moira said.

"Did your boyfriend put the mattress on top?"

Moira nodded, not willing to trust her own voice.

"He should've used more cords. It's about to fall off. If you'll step out, I'll help you secure it. How much farther are you going?"

"There's a motel down the road," Moira said. "A friend is meeting us. She's going to drive us to her house, but she says it's hard to get to without GPS."

The cop smiled. It made her seem younger. She stepped back so that Moira could open the door. She did, and got out, her knees cracking as she stood.

Back in Beatty, she'd checked her clothes for blood. She hoped she checked well enough because right now, it felt like she was covered.

"When'd you lose your job?" the cop asked softly.

"At the Mirage?" Moira asked.

The cop was looking up at the mattress. The fucking thing had tilted toward the driver's side, and looked like it was going to fall off.

Moira glanced at the cop's name badge. Foster.

"No," the cop said. "In Wisconsin. When'd you lose your job there?"

"Oh." Moira reached up and pushed the mattress back toward the roof of the van. The mattress was hot and smelled faintly of mold. "About a year ago. We were out of money."

She was out of money. She hadn't known Kasey yet.

The cop reached up and helped push. "Tough stuff. It's amazing you got a job in this economy."

Moira shoved. The mattress slid. Then she grabbed the edge of a bungee cord and pulled, praying it wouldn't snap.

"It was a long shot. I called and lied. I said I was coming to Vegas and could he give me part-time work? And it turned out someone had just quit and he didn't want to hire people because so many showed up...."

She trailed off. She'd learned a lot over the years. Don't lie unless you could help it and even in the middle of your lies, tell a little truth. She mixed what she had learned from the news with the fact that she hadn't worked for more than a year—not because she got laid off, but because she didn't have to.

"You need one more cord," the cop said.

"I don't have one," Moira said. "I'm only going a few more miles."

"Then you're going to follow your friend," the cop said. God, she paid attention to everything.

"Maybe she'll have the cash to buy another cord," Moira said, letting herself sound as tired as she felt.

The cop studied her again, then gave her a rueful smile. "Find out if she has enough for some lotion for that sunburn, too."

Then the cop nodded, and headed back to her car. Moira pushed at the mattress, made sure the other cord was tight, and gave a little wave as the cop drove around her.

Moira knew the ploy. Drive a few yards ahead, watch to see if the woman lied.

But Moira wasn't lying, not about meeting someone at a motel, and that would be enough for the cop.

Moira's hands shook as she let herself back into the car. She leaned her head back and closed her eyes for a moment. It was damn hot inside.

"You okay?" Kasey asked.

"Fine," Moira said and sat up. She turned the key in the ignition, started the car, and let the AC come back on. Even though it didn't work well, it worked well enough.

Five minutes.

Five fucking hassle-free minutes.

That's all she asked.

Five minutes and a little time to get out of this place.

Nothing more.

— 32 —

The Hawthorne Police Department was nothing like the LAPD. Not in structure, not in hierarchy, and certainly not in numbers. For one thing, the entire Hawthorne PD was located in one building—one small building that would fit comfortably in a seedy strip mall in Van Nuys. No public relations department, no fiefdoms, no tactical, no nothing.

Just a few guys with some badges and guns. Sure, they'd gone to a police academy somewhere, usually spent a rookie year somewhere else—either Reno or Carson City or Vegas, and then decided that small town life was better.

A few were military police who retired and moved over, thinking the job was the same. And a few were local boys, raised in Hawthorne, familiar with the town, its history and traditions, and its skeletons.

Cahill avoided them. The skeletons, the history and tradition, and the local boys. Sometimes he had a beer with the former MPs, swapping war stories—theirs from actual wars, and his from the streets of LA.

They had a mutual respect, him and the MPs. Everyone else at Hawthorne PD, in his not-so-humble opinion, were strictly amateurs.

Which was why they didn't notice when he came back to the department in a different mood—a foul mood, yes, but murder never put anyone in a good mood. His mood was jumpy, odd, furtive, a bit guilty. He hated it, but Dirksen brought that out in him.

Too many memories. Too many things he'd done wrong.

The department smelled of old coffee, bad air conditioning, and dust. The whole town smelled of dust because the wind never stopped blowing, blowing that reddish desert sand all over everything. Sometimes he wondered what he was inhaling with the wind—some chemical weapon now decommissioned? A bit of radiation?—but mostly he tried not to think about it.

Right now, he didn't want to think about anything, except that guy who peeled out of the neighborhood, speeding away from Storvick's house.

Cahill sat at his desk, and as he did, the chief came over with a printout.

"I've got enough on my plate," Cahill snapped. Probably not wise to yell at the boss, no matter how rinky-dink you thought he was, but Cahill was in no mood for moderation.

"I think this is part of your plate," the chief said, and walked away.

Cahill picked up the printout. Police report from Tonopah, just filed. Man found shot behind a dumpster. Owned a car parked more than a block away. A car filled with laptops, surveillance equipment, extra change of clothes, and more than one cell phone.

Man was shot twice with a .38.

"Fuck," Cahill said. "We have a spree."

— 33 —

The motel looked sleazier than she remembered, not the kind of place a hard-up mother would take her child unless the hard-up mother wanted to hook for a little extra cash. No wonder the cop had looked at her funny when she mentioned a motel farther down Boulder Highway.

At least Moira hadn't mentioned which motel.

But as far as she could tell, the cop hadn't followed her here, either.

Still, she parked at the far end of the parking lot, away from Boulder Highway. If the cop came looking, she'd see the van, but she'd have to look for it.

And maybe by the time she thought of it, Moira would be long gone.

She scanned the lot, saw the SUV that Analyn had mentioned, confirmed the plate number, and let out a small sigh of relief. She got out, opened the back door of the van, and started to unbuckle Kasey.

"Is my mom here?" Kasey asked.

"Yes," Moira said, bracing herself for the squeal of joy, the struggle as Kasey tried to run to her.

Instead, Kasey looked militant. She didn't move from the seat. "Can I stay here?"

"In the motel?" Moira asked. Kasey had never been concerned about motels before.

Kasey shook her head. "Here."

Moira's heart sank. The kid didn't want to see her mom. Maybe Kasey was just afraid. Maybe she was scared it was all a trick.

Moira should comfort her, but Moira wasn't the comforting type.

"No, you can't stay here," Moira said, and lifted her out of the seat.

Kasey clung to the Barbie. Her body twisted. "Don't wanna go."

Dammit. Moira did not need a scene outside. "Why not?"

Kasey's lips closed hard and she looked away.

"Tell me why not," Moira said as she set Kasey on the ground, "or you're coming with me."

"She told him to take me," Kasey whispered.

Moira froze. "Your mother told who to take you?"

"*Him.*" Kasey still wasn't looking at Moira. Kasey wasn't really looking at anything.

"Your father?" Moira asked.

Kasey nodded once, a brief, almost invisible movement.

God, Kasey believed this. No wonder she wasn't interested in her mom. As if Moira would bring her to a woman who had given her kid to that scum. Moira knew better. But how could she convince Kasey?

Kasey, who really and truly believed the worst.

"Son of a bitch," Moira said, and wondered what the hell to do next.

— 34 —

A spree killer was a slightly different animal than a serial killer. Cahill had caught a few low-level serials in his day, mostly careless guys who went from community to community in the LA Basin, and would've been caught had they worked a smaller city. Low-level serials were often disorganized and lousy, leaving tons of evidence on the scene. They were hard to catch only when they moved jurisdictions—like states or in places like LA where the cops from different precincts snubbed each other and didn't look at the memos.

Cahill looked around the station. A few uniforms, the chief, the dispatch in her own special room. (Just one dispatch, because this was a low crime area, thanks to the military. He still shook his head over that. Just one dispatch per shift, which was really two more dispatches than the community needed, considering how few calls came in requesting police assistance.) Everyone was bent over a desk or a computer or talking into a cell.

No one had heard his outburst, or if they had, they hadn't understood it.

They didn't realize just how damn dangerous a spree killer could be.

Serials killed as part of a compulsion, one that usually showed up in childhood. The media had been filled with information about serials for years, and most of the information was right: the insensitive and violent child who went from mutilating small animals to killing them, to injuring friends and family, to killing someone familiar usually somewhere near home, to figuring out how to kill more and more without getting caught.

A serial first identified their compulsion as a hobby. Then it became a profession of sorts, a career, something to be proud of. Only the most self-aware called it a compulsion, and somewhere along the way, rationalized the compulsion away, usually in a form of egotism (*I'm good at this, so therefore I should do it*).

The spree killer was all about rage. Sudden, uncontrollable rage, started by a precipitating event: a "snap," as the pop psychologists called it. The guy who murdered that fashion designer Versace in the 1990s had been a spree killer, just like Richard Speck who murdered all the nurses in Chicago in the 1960s had been. Just like Charles Starkweather in the 1950s, who was identified as the first spree killer, although Cahill always doubted that was true. There just hadn't been a mass media to out the spree killers before that.

Not that there were a lot of them.

Or at least, there might not have been a lot of them. They often got argued about. Some called the DC snipers of 2002 spree killers, but others didn't. They were something else, some said, because they worked as a pair, and because no one could find the precipitating event.

Cahill always thought the older DC sniper guy was a spree. He'd been pretty buttoned together until his personal situation disintegrated. Then he went to war—war against a made-up enemy, but war just the same.

Just like every other spree Cahill had read about.

Of course, you couldn't decide on a spree with just two pieces of evidence.

He picked up the phone, called the number for the Tonopah PD. That there was a Tonopah PD surprised the hell out of him. Wasn't that place the closest thing to a ghost town?

When a single guy answered with his name and rank, Cahill felt vindicated. A "department" so small that the cops used cell phones instead of a dispatch. There probably was one guy per shift, and that guy was underemployed.

Cahill identified himself, and asked about the body.

"White male, forties, muscular. Identification says he's Steven Davis. Fixed address is in California, but I can't raise anybody there, and my calls all go to his cell."

Strange, Cahill thought. But stranger that the man's description fit the description of the guy the ghouls had seen near Storvick's house.

"You seen him before?" Cahill asked.

"You kidding?" the cop said. "He was driving through. Weird thing, though."

"What?" Cahill asked.

"He parked off the highway, behind one of our buildings."

"So?" Cahill asked.

"So no one gets off the highway. This desert scares most people." The cop said that last like most people were idiots. Like Cahill would understand.

Cahill did understand. The desert was damn dangerous, and most people had no clue what they were heading into when they went south of Hawthorne. Most of them survived because their cars were tuned and they didn't run out of gas and there weren't a lot of predators dumb enough to take these roads.

"Where was he killed?"

"In behind Decker's Market," the cop said. "Now, everybody driving through stops at Decker's Market. It's like a way station for the panicked. They see a gas pump, an Open sign, and they stock up like there's no tomorrow."

"Did he stop there?" Cahill ask.

"He never went in."

"Anyone in the market hear the shots?"

"No," the cop said.

Cahill frowned. "Should they have heard it?"

"Oh, yeah. Happened just a few feet from the door. Should've sounded like an explosion."

"I trust the state police are taking this," Cahill said, not caring if he offended the cop.

"You better believe it. I don't have this kind of training," the cop said.

"You find the gun?" Cahill asked.

"It wasn't anywhere obvious," the cop said.

"Says here the body was behind the Dumpster. Did you look inside?"

"Not really," the cop said, sounding that note of disgust. "I figured it'd be better to have the crime scene guys look."

"You think the gun was there?" Cahill asked.

"No," the cop said. "The body'd been moved. There were bloody drag marks. But I can't imagine someone who was that careful would hide the gun in the Dumpster."

"Doesn't sound like someone is being careful," Cahill said. "You don't leave a body in the open if you're being careful."

"I guess," the cop said, with that tone most people used when they were too polite to disagree.

Cahill had had enough. "Anything else unusual?"

"No," the cop said. "Just random tourists, stopping as they drove to Vegas."

"Random tourists," Cahill repeated. "Anyone there about the time the guy got shot?"

"Just a woman and a kid," the cop said. "The Truscotts were worried that they wouldn't make it to Vegas."

"Who're the Truscotts?" Cahill asked.

"The owners of Decker's Market. It's been in Amber's family since the boom."

"The boom?"

"The mining boom, damn near a hundred years ago now. Most of the folks here have been here for a very long time."

The cop made it sound like they'd all been there since the mining boom. Cahill shuddered just a little. He'd driven through Tonopah and, he realized from the cop's description, he'd even stopped at Decker's Market. He'd never live in that place—not for one year, let alone for his entire life.

Hawthorne was too small for him. He couldn't imagine living in Tonopah.

"This woman," he said, "she hear anything?"

"She was gone before I got there," the cop said. "She was gone before Garth found the body."

"So how come the Truscotts were worried about her?" Cahill asked.

"Because of her van," the cop said.

Cahill felt cold. "A van with a mattress on top?"

"Yeah," the cop said. "I guess it was old and didn't look very sturdy. The little girl was a charmer and the woman was sunburned, and they were afraid she might not make it to Vegas."

"They get any clue as to her identity?" Cahill asked.

"I thought of that," the cop said. "I asked because I was hoping she'd be a witness."

Cahill waited.

"But she paid in cash, and she didn't say a lot about herself."

"What about the little girl?" Cahill asked.

"What about her?"

"Did she say anything?"

"No," the cop said. "They just stopped, got a few things, and left."

"Do you think they saw the guy?" Cahill asked.

"I doubt it," the cop said. "I'm sure they would've reported it."

Maybe not, Cahill thought, but didn't say.

One of the ghouls—the kid—had mentioned the van. It couldn't be a coincidence. And the driver had actually gone into Storvick's house.

"You think you can give me the Truscotts' phone number?" Cahill asked. "I've got a few questions."

"Sure," the cop said, and rattled off a number. "I'll walk on over there and let them know you're going to call. You be nice to them, you hear? They're pretty shook up."

"I bet they are," Cahill said, and hung up.

— 35 —

Moira looked at the door into the motel, only a few yards away. She and Kasey couldn't stay out here. Moira had felt exposed ever since she shot that guy in Tonopah.

"What do you want me to do with you, then?" Moira asked Kasey.

Kasey looked at her for the first time since lodging the protest. Had no one ever listened to this girl before?

Probably not. Or at least, not since she had been in the custody of *him*.

"Can I stay with you?" Kasey asked softly.

Moira's eyebrows went up. No one had ever asked to be with her before. Not in this deep, serious way.

And she'd been thinking about it. She could use Kasey. They could be a team. Kasey already had the wave down. And that devastating "bye-bye." Kasey would be good.

But she'd live on the road, and at some point, Moira really would have to take care of her. The kind of emotional care that Moira wasn't capable of. The kind Kasey seemed to want right now.

"Tell you what," Moira said, not quite willing to say *no*. "We'll go see your mom. If she can't change your mind, you can leave with me."

Which was damn near a commitment. After all, Moira wasn't going to put anyone into the system no matter what. No kid deserved that. Not for any reason. Especially a kid like Kasey, with that brain and the cold "bye-bye."

"Okay," Kasey said and extended her hand. Trusting. More trusting than she had ever been.

Moira took her hand and led her inside the motel. It was cool in the reception area—if you could call the space that was the same size as a 1950s hotel room a reception area. There was a desk and an office behind it, plus a few chairs and a small sofa under the window, but that was it. You couldn't squeeze a lot of people in here if you tried.

"I'm here to meet Anna Nevins," Moira said, using the alias she had told Analyn to use. "She said I could get the room number from you."

The guy behind the desk, rabbity, dark, probably unemployable anywhere else, nodded, and said, "Fourteen."

So much for privacy. Someone really should tell the motel's owners how easy it would be attack a woman in this place. The doors were thin, the windows easy-access, and the damn counterman didn't really care who knew where his guests were.

"Did she leave me a key?" Moira asked, keeping her voice calm.

"No," he said. "But she's there now. Out the door to your left."

Je-*sus*. Easy as pie to take her out. Fortunately they wouldn't be there long. And fortunately, Kasey was with Moira. Otherwise this guy just might get what-for.

Moira looked at Kasey. The girl looked up at her, expectantly. See? She even kept Moira calm when Moira needed to be calm.

"Thanks," Moira said, and headed out of the reception area. She went out the door and to her left as instructed, Kasey's hand clamped tightly in her own.

Goddamn kid, tempting her like that. Goddamn kid, actually having an influence on her. Goddamn kid, making her feel something.

No one had done that in a very, very long time.

— 36 —

They sounded young and scared and shaken. Cahill listened, phone pressed between his shoulder and ear, as the man—who sounded more like a teenager—described finding the body.

Cahill was glad that the department was quiet. Only a few uniforms filing reports, the chief back in his office. The clack-clack of computer keys was the only sound around him, which was good. Because the boy—whose name was Garth Truscott—had put him on speaker.

Cahill was listening to Truscott and his wife Amber. Cahill could hear some tinny music, a radio station from Vegas, playing what was now called Adult Contemporary. Some rustling as someone moved bags or papers.

Then a baby fussed.

"Shh, Saylor," Amber cooed. "Mommy and Daddy are on the phone."

A baby. Jesus. No wonder they were freaked out.

They had a kid in that store, and someone had been shot outside.

Cahill leaned his chair back, caught the phone's receiver, and held it in his hand, pressing it as hard against his ear as he could. He'd stopped at that store more than once, and barely remembered it. Dust-covered, like most of central and southern Nevada. Isolated. Windows everywhere. The highway too close, not that it mattered, since there was never any traffic.

He wondered if that was the first time anyone had been murdered in Tonopah in recent memory. He wasn't going to ask—not these kids, anyway. Maybe the cop. Maybe the state police.

Truscott's voice shook as he described the body. The description was word-for-word the same as the cop's, which Cahill did not find suspicious. The kid had seen it, the cop dutifully reported it. The only difference was that Truscott's voice was a little more flat, filled with shock still, shock and fear and worry that someone might come to get him.

Cahill didn't reassure him. It wasn't his job to calm two kids out of their element in Tonopah.

"So," he said, "tell me about the woman with the van."

"Why?" Amber asked.

"Because she might have seen something," he said. "She was there when the guy was shot, right?"

"We don't know when he was shot," Truscott said.

"But you do know roughly, right?"

"Yes," Amber said. "I make Garth take out Saylor's diapers after I change her. We don't want this place smelling of poo."

Cahill paused for a moment, the word "poo" stopping him. Who said that these days? How young were these two and why were they running a store? Why were they stuck in Tonopah? Were they stuck because they had to take care of that baby and her—his?—poo?

And they named the baby Saylor. In the desert. Did they realize the irony? Or was it a metaphor? Or just a bit of hope—thinking maybe the baby would get away since they no longer could.

"So when did you take out the trash?" Cahill asked.

"I told you," Truscott said. "I found him at—"

"I mean before," Cahill said.

"Oh." Truscott paused. "About an hour before."

"And there was no body."

"No," Truscott said. "I would've noticed."

"Are you sure?"

146

"He was hard to miss. Blood was everywhere. It was awful. And his feet were sticking out."

"Did you see anyone unusual near the store?" Cahill asked.

"What do you mean unusual?" Amber asked. Her voice was breathless. He wished he could see her, figure out if she was as wispy as her voice or fat and discouraged or just plain dumb. He couldn't tell, not even if he closed his eyes and imagined himself there instead of this damn department he'd trapped himself in.

"I mean, did you see anyone you hadn't seen before? I can't say more than that. You know what's unusual in Tonopah. I don't."

His tone was harsher than he had planned. One of the uniforms glanced over at him. Apparently, Cahill's irritated voice had carried all the way across the room.

"We get strange people all the time," the girl said. "We try not to think about it."

Clearly she tried not to think about. He could feel her fear, radiating through the phone.

"Has something like this happened before?" he asked.

"A shooting?" She sounded shocked. "No."

"We're a really small town," Truscott said, as if he felt the need to apologize.

"You'd notice if there were strangers," Cahill said.

"Yes," Truscott said.

"So no one came in with the dead guy," Cahill said.

"If they did, they left with someone else," Truscott said.

Cahill made a note of that. He'd tell the state police to make sure no one else had been in the dead guy's car.

"And you didn't see anyone else beside the woman in the van between the times you took out the garbage," Cahill said.

"No one," Truscott said.

"Would they have stopped somewhere else?" Cahill asked.

"We have a diner," Amber said. "And a few fast food places. You could check with them."

He was sure someone would, but he wasn't going to burn up the phone lines on it. Not with this van in his sights. "So tell me about the woman."

"I told her to buy some aloe," the girl said. "She was really sunburned."

"Did she buy the aloe?" Cahill asked.

"Yes," the girl said. "She bought that and sunscreen for her daughter."

"Anything else about her?"

"She paid cash," Truscott said. "All wadded up from her pocket. Like she only had a little bit and she was hoarding it."

Interesting that Truscott had noticed that detail. Interesting that she acted poor. But she was driving a van that was in terrible condition with a mattress on top. Maybe she was what she appeared to be—a woman down on her luck.

"It was the little girl I was worried about," Amber said.

"Why?" Cahill asked.

"She was so quiet. I was afraid maybe she had heat stroke or something, but she wasn't too hot. I checked."

"You touched her?" Cahill asked, amazed that a mother would let a stranger touch her child.

"Yeah," Amber said. "When her mom went to get something from the van. I just had to see. If she was too hot, I would've called our doc and made them stay at least until sundown. You'd be surprised how much heat stroke we get here, and how deadly it is. People have attacks in the desert, and they die out there."

It took Cahill a moment to realize she was done. "Let me get this straight," he said. "The woman went outside."

"Yes," Amber said.

"By herself," he said.

"Yes." Amber sounded different as if she had moved her head, probably looking at her husband for confirmation.

"Did she look different when she came back?" he asked.

"Different how?" Truscott asked, clearly taking over for his wife.

"Upset, angry?"

"No," he said. "If anything, she seemed even more tired."

"But she had changed her shoes," Amber said.

"She had?" Cahill hadn't expected that detail.

"She took a while outside, and when she came in, she said she broke a strap on her shoe, and she pointed to her flip-flops. I got the sense it had taken a while to find them."

Fuck. Shoe prints. That woman was brilliant. There was a fresh blood trail. She might have stepped in it—probably had, if she was the one who dragged the guy to the Dumpster. And she didn't want to track the blood into the store. Instead, she'd walked to her van, changed shoes, and come back to the store, calm as hell.

But not that calm. She admitted to changing shoes, afraid the other woman would notice.

An unplanned kill?

If that was the case, then Storvick was planned.

So who was the guy following her? And who was the kid?

"She was a bitty thing," the girl said. "I don't think she could've killed him."

"You saw the body?" Cahill asked.

There was a pause, as if they were both ashamed of that. But people always slowed down for an accident. The more grisly and gruesome something was, the more people wanted to see.

"I didn't believe Garth," she whispered.

"It's okay," Cahill said.

"He didn't want me to go outside."

"But you did," Cahill said.

"That guy was big," Amber said, as confirmation. "Looked strong. Military. I can't believe she could've killed him. He didn't look like the kind of guy you could take by surprise."

"So he was young, then?" Cahill asked, feeling disappointed. He'd been thinking this was the guy who peeled out of the neighborhood. But her description sounded off.

"No, no," she said. "He was as old as my dad, like forty or something."

"His hair was too long to be military," Truscott said. "Maybe a cop or something, but not military."

"But he was big, athletic," Amber said. "He had to weigh a lot. I couldn't've dragged him."

You could've if he'd threatened your baby and you killed him, Cahill nearly said. Sometimes size didn't matter at all.

"So, an in-shape middle-aged guy," Cahill said. "Forty-something."

Just like the old woman had said on the street.

"I couldn't've killed him," Amber said. "He'd've stopped me in a minute."

Or not. Cahill didn't expect little women with kids to be a threat unless he went after the kid or the woman was a meth addict or something. He wouldn't have had his guard up. If this guy was a cop or ex-military, he wouldn't have had his guard up either.

"Did she call her daughter by name?" he asked, reaching. He needed more than the van and the mattress and the sunburn.

"No," Truscott said. "She called her honey or something like that."

"Babe," Amber said. "She called her babe."

"Like she was hiding something?" Cahill asked.

"Like she always called her that," Amber said. "You think she did something, that woman?"

Cahill wasn't going to discuss his suspicions with them anymore than he already had.

"I think she saw something. I think she was pretty calm about it, determined to get her daughter out of there."

"She could've told us," Amber said. "I mean, we have a baby here, and everything. It's only fair."

Her sudden vehemence took his breath away. He hadn't expected it.

"You're right," he said. "Tell the state police that when they come. Give them everything they need to find her."

"You think we're going to be safe?" Truscott asked, his voice wobbling again.

"I think you'll be just fine," Cahill lied, then he hung up. He had a lot to do here, but first he had to find out some information.

"Hey," he said, leaning back in his chair. Two uniforms looked up, young guys looking for promotions. Exactly what Cahill needed.

Both of them looked at him expectantly.

"Either one of you good at computers?" he asked.

The guy to his right nodded. What was the kid's name? Inman? Engram? Cahill squinted. The name embroidered on the uniform proved him half right. Ingram. Daniel Ingram. That's right. The kid was always fiddling with the latest gadget.

"I need you to search the western half of the U.S., looking for murders with a variation on these details." He listed the gun, the van, the description of the dead men. He almost added the blond woman, but then thought maybe she was a ringer. Or maybe she and the girl were part of the killer's family. Three people instead of two, but causing as much confusion as the DC snipers initially did. "I want to know if there's a pattern. I'm especially interested in a geographical pattern."

"Geographical pattern?" Ingram asked, which immediately made Cahill wonder if he was up to the job.

"He wants to know if the killings were on a set route," said the other uniform with a bit of contempt in his voice.

"Exactly," Cahill said. "I need information as soon as you can confirm it."

"What's going on?" Ingram asked.

"Maybe nothing," Cahill said. "Just do the job."

The kid nodded and went to the only truly fast computer in the place—the one near the chief's office, a communal thing that an actual tech cleaned of viruses each and every day.

"You," Cahill said to the other uniform. "What's your name again?"

Because the guy's name was impossible for Cahill to see from this distance. "Jason Dodd," the guy said like he was offended Cahill didn't remember.

"Well, Dodd, I have an assignment for you, too. Put out an APB on this van, with this description of the driver." Then Cahill frowned. There was a kid in the vehicle. Should he make it an AMBER Alert?

"What van? What driver?" Dodd asked.

Cahill's frown got deeper. AMBERs were valuable tools. If he was wrong, if that was truly some woman who had the misfortune to get into the middle of all of this, then it would be his badge.

"Let me tell you," he said, and heaved himself out of the chair.

He'd catch the woman if nothing else, and maybe she would have information for Dirksen. And maybe that would be enough to get Dirksen off his back.

Maybe.

If he was lucky.

— 37 —

The knock made her start, even though she was expecting it, even though she was hoping for it. Analyn leapt to her feet, her heart pounding. She glanced at the TV showing troops in Afghanistan, a crawl beneath, the voice belonging to that CNN woman, the one with the accent.

Analyn didn't remember turning to CNN. She didn't remember much after she got in the room, except being scared.

Scared nothing would happen, no one would come.

The knock sounded again.

She smoothed her hair, hoped—prayed—that Kasey was out there.

Analyn crossed the few feet of thin carpet to the door, didn't look into the peephole because she wouldn't recognize Moira if she saw her, and she would be able to see down to Kasey.

Analyn pulled the door open, and there was her daughter. Taller, thinner. Beautiful.

She held the hand of a sunburned woman with dead eyes. That woman looked more like Kasey's mom than Analyn did. Same white-blond hair, same delicate features. They almost looked like the same person—one the child and the other all grown up.

"Kasey," Analyn breathed. She crouched and opened her arms.

Kasey cringed behind the woman's leg.

"I'm Moira," the woman said. "It's hot out here. Can we come in?"

Her flat tone—so reassuring on the phone—was scary here. She carried big purse and she seemed *off* somehow. Analyn couldn't figure out how.

She stood, her face warming—and not from the heat. From her daughter's rejection.

Analyn moved away from the door. "Yes, yes," she said. "Please do come in."

Moira did, but she had to pull Kasey along.

"What's wrong with her?" Analyn asked Moira.

"Aside from being abused by a pedophile, and then watching him get shot right in front of her? Nothing really," Moira said.

Analyn's breath caught. What had this woman been saying to her daughter?

"I want to go," Kasey said.

Analyn's mouth was dry. Kasey was looking at Moira, not Analyn. Kasey wanted to leave with this very scary woman.

"Honey," Analyn said. "It's Mommy."

Kasey looked up at her, eyes glistening. "I know."

Analyn looked at Moira in panic. "What's going on?"

Moira shrugged. "Don't ask me. Ask Kasey."

"Honey, I hired Moira to get you," Analyn said. "She saved you, and brought you to me."

"No," Kasey said.

No? How could Kasey say *no* to that? It was true.

"She thinks you gave her to your husband," Moira said.

"What?" Analyn couldn't believe that. Why would Kasey think something like that?

But the police had. They had checked her out, discovered she was clean. Hell, the company that Moira worked for—Dealmakers—had investigated her, too. They didn't want to get involved in something that was strictly domestic.

Which this wasn't.

SPREE

But Analyn couldn't tell if Moira believed it. Was that why the woman was so reserved, so flat?

"Of course, I didn't give you to him." Analyn crouched again. Kasey cringed, but Analyn didn't care. "I came home from work and you and your stuff were gone. So was Jolene."

"Who's Jolene?" Moira asked.

"The sitter," Analyn said, looking up at her. "He paid her off, the bastard. She went to jail for taking part in a kidnapping. They couldn't find him."

"You told him to come," Kasey said from behind Moira's leg. "You told him it was okay."

"No, baby," Analyn said, pleading. "I would never have done that. I was hiding you from him."

She'd legally changed her name, gotten new credit cards in the name of a corporation she'd founded, hid them both as best she could without completely disappearing. She never thought Royce would be smart enough to find her.

But he had.

And he had taken Kasey.

She had thought her nightmare would end this afternoon, but it was still continuing.

"I didn't tell him to get you. Don't you remember running away from him in the middle of the night?"

Kasey's head tilted. Analyn knew that look, even on Kasey's older features. Nine months—as long as she carried her inside—that's how long they had been separated.

Nine months. What had that bastard done to her in nine months?

"Remember I told you we had a new name, and we shouldn't ever mention Daddy? Remember?"

Kasey bit her lower lip. "He said…."

He said. *He* said. Goddamn that bastard. He'd lied to her, poisoned her, done God knows what to her, and made her believe that no one loved her.

That fucking bastard.

155

But Analyn didn't say any of that out loud. She was afraid her anger would scare her child.

Her precious, damaged child.

"He lied, honey," Analyn said.

Kasey's lip trembled even more. Her eyes were filled with tears. "You didn't come."

"I didn't know where you were."

"He said you didn't want me."

"I wanted you so much I went to the police every day. I hired people. I found Moira. She got you, didn't she? She brought you to me."

Kasey stared at her. This child was not the child who left. This child didn't trust her.

This child probably didn't trust anyone, and that broke Analyn's heart.

Then Kasey looked up at Moira. "That true?"

"Yes," Moira said.

"How do you know?" Shaking voice, her entire body closed in on itself.

Analyn would've picked her up, but Moira didn't. She didn't even crouch. She just looked down on her with the same flat gaze she'd had since she came in the door.

"I checked," Moira said. "I had to make sure your mom was on the level. I'm not the kind of person who takes children from bad guys and gives them to other bad guys."

Kasey nodded. A tear ran down her cheek. "Okay."

Analyn waited. This was a crucial moment, and she sensed that if she spoke, she'd ruin it.

"You gonna hug your mom?" Moira asked.

"No," Kasey said, but she wasn't cringing any more. She looked at Analyn like a tired child looked at a blanket and pillow.

"But you're going with her," Moira said, and that wasn't a question.

Even Kasey knew it wasn't a question. Another tear ran down her cheek.

"Can I?" she whispered, not to Moira, but to Analyn.

"Do you want to?" Analyn asked, scared the answer would be *no*. If the answer was *no*, what would she do? What could she do?

"Yes," Kasey said.

And Analyn let out a sigh of relief.

"Can Moira come?" Kasey asked.

"Sure," Analyn said, as Moira said, "No."

Kasey and Analyn looked at Moira.

She shrugged, her eyes softer than they had been, her face not quite as rigid. Analyn almost had the sense she was sad.

"I don't do families," she said, looking at Kasey.

"Please?" Kasey asked.

Moira shook her head. "You don't want me. I'll remind you of the bad stuff."

"You're not bad," Kasey said.

"Ah, babe," Moira said. "You really don't know that."

"I do," Kasey said.

"You're not," Analyn said, not wanting to disillusion her daughter. "You're her savior."

Moira made a small sound of dismissal, then shook her head. "Well, let's get me out of here then before I mess that up, too. Her stuff is in my van. We gotta get it out."

Analyn had a sense that the afternoon was getting away from her. She hadn't expected this. She had expected hugs and tears and lots of relief. Not a flat-faced woman and a sad little girl who looked like her Kasey but didn't at the same time.

Analyn told herself she had to be thankful Kasey was here—and she *was*—but she was scared, too. This was a lot bigger than she ever imagined, a lot harder.

Happy endings only existed in the movies.

This was just the beginning of something else, something different. Something brand new.

— 38 —

Cahill spent the next fifteen minutes on the phone with the state police, making certain he would remain in the loop on the Tonopah case. The state police hadn't even arrived in Tonopah yet, and Cahill was delaying them further. He wanted someone good on this, someone who actually had some experience with tough characters.

That was what he said. *Tough characters.*

But he meant mobsters.

He got up from his desk after that call and walked over to the small kitchen someone had set up back when the building was built. An ancient refrigerator chugged, on damn close to its last legs. The giant microwave dated from the 1980s and probably gave off as much radiation as the stuff hidden in the Depot.

He poured himself a cup of coffee—which usually was okay here, since the chief liked to spring for the good stuff at a nearby grocery store. Cahill took a carton of milk out of the fridge, sniffed the cardboard, decided that the milk hadn't gone bad yet, and added it to his coffee.

Then he walked back to his desk.

He hoped the state police had understood him. He didn't want to bring up the words *mob* or *mobsters*, because then he'd get The Speech. He'd probably heard The Speech two hundred times since he moved to Nevada.

The mob no longer ran Nevada. The mob was long gone. The mob was once influential, but had been defanged long ago.

Like those guys would ever entirely go away.

Cahill knew they were mostly gone—at least the old-time ones, the ones interested in gambling and politics and assassination. The mob remained here and in Los Angeles and in Chicago and New York and Florida, but that mob focused on drugs and hookers and turf wars within its own borders. That mob wasn't bright enough to handle something as complex as a modern casino, and not organized enough to get involved in modern politics.

But he wanted to give the state police a heads-up about Dirksen without mentioning his name. Without mentioning the prior connection. Without really getting involved.

Because he didn't want Dirksen to know he was talking about him, and he didn't want the state police to think Cahill knew something about him.

He needed to stay as clean as he could on this, and maybe, just maybe, he could get Dirksen off his back.

After all, the dead guy in Tonopah might put the whole case on the state police and Dirksen would go to the guys he'd bought off there.

Sure, and forget about Storvick and the money. Which Cahill hadn't even started investigating.

"Hey, Detective, c'mere." Ingram waved him over to the computer.

Cahill sighed inwardly. This uniform had at least called him *detective*, but he could've brought the information to Cahill's desk. That's what would've happened at the LAPD, unless the uniform had been playing some kind of game.

But no one really played games here in Hawthorne, except maybe Cahill himself. He sighed and carried his rapidly cooling coffee over to the computer desk.

"What?" he said in a tone that implied Ingram had better have found something or he would piss Cahill off.

Ingram caught the tone. He shrugged forward just a little. "Two hits, unsolved, both regional. Some departments are putting public details of their unsolveds on this national database, it's not FBI, but—"

"I know," Cahill said. He'd checked it himself back in LA, back when it seemed like every transient killer in the world ended up in California. In fact, he'd been one of the guys arguing for a national database of un-solveds back in the 1990s, when rumors started about a trucker killing people near the interstates. He hadn't stuck around enough to know if that evolved from rumor to fact, but he remembered how frustrated he felt, confined to California databases only.

"Okay," Ingram said, seemingly unfazed by Cahill's tone. "The first is in Lincoln. A guy gets shot—"

"Lincoln, Nebraska?" Cahill asked, trying to be clear.

"Yes," Ingram said as if there was no other Lincoln on the planet. "A guy got shot in the chest, twice, with a .38. The guy was pretty much a loner, except that evening, a neighbor saw a van parked outside, and the van had a mattress on the roof, Wisconsin plates."

"Anyone see the woman or the little girl?"

"A little girl. That's what made the neighbor call 911. Because the guy who was killed, he was on one of those sex predator lists. He wasn't sup-posed to be within blocks of a little kid."

Cahill felt a shiver of anticipation run through him. This did have promise. "And?"

"And when the cops showed up, no van, but they found the body. They figured that someone killed him to save the kid, and while they of-ficially have the case open, they're not really trying that hard to solve it, you know what I mean?"

Cahill did know. Sometimes the bad guys did the job for you. Some-times it was just better to have the scum scraped off the face of the earth than it was to go after the person who did the scraping.

"Print that for me." Cahill hated reading on-screen. "You said you have one more?"

"Salt Lake City. Mid-morning, a van with a mattress on top nearly topples over making the corner out of this apartment complex. Wiscon-sin plates. A guy actually pulled up next to the van at the next light, and asked it to pull over, which the driver—a woman—does. He helps her tighten the mattress on top, and sends her on her way. She seems a bit spooked, but he blames it on the kid in the back, figures she's down on her luck and trying to get away from something bad."

"Someone put this in the unsolved database?" Cahill asked.

"Only because a day later, someone reports liquid dripping from the ceiling of the apartment above. Turns out the liquid is blood that seeped through the floor and was dripping down. The guy who lived up there had been shot twice in the chest. That's when the cops canvassed and the only person who hadn't belonged in the neighborhood was the woman in the van."

"That seems flimsy," Cahill said.

"It would have been, except this guy was one of those Internet predators, and they figured he'd gone after the woman or the kid. Someone had downloaded his database after he died and made a copy of everything. The Salt Lake City cops figure some stuff got deleted, probably pictures of the woman or the kid."

Cahill frowned. Storvick was a rapist. The guy in Lincoln a sexual predator of some kind, and then this. That tied them together loosely, and the woman in the van had been near them—not really trying to hide. But it didn't exactly make sense.

Unless she was tracking down a network of child pornographers or something. But why bring the kid with her?

"We confiscated Storvick's computer, right?" he asked.

"Yes, sir."

"Go over it. I'll bet you find some things you won't want to see." Then Cahill paused, remembering the two cell phones on the body. "And check to see what he was doing with those cell phones."

"You think this is all linked?" Ingram asked.

"Don't you?" Cahill asked.

"It does seem strange, sir," Ingram said.

"Keep digging. See what else you can find," Cahill said. "And print me up both cases."

"Will do," Ingram said.

Cahill went back to his desk. A female vigilante, going after sexual predators. Really? Was that even possible? If so, why would she be so visible?

Or was someone after her, someone torturing the people she talked to and then killing them after she left?

Or was it something else, something stranger than that?

And what was she doing with the kid?

For the first time since he moved to Hawthorne, a case intrigued him. He sipped his now-cold coffee and paged through the first file. Lincoln, Nebraska, and Salt Lake City, Utah, were both on Interstate 80. If someone was driving west from Wisconsin, they'd either take Interstate 90 to the north or take Interstate 35 down to Des Moines and catch Interstate 80.

If you were deliberately heading to Hawthorne—and why else come here, especially from Wisconsin? It certainly wasn't the best route to Vegas, particularly with a kid in the van—then Interstate 80 was the most direct route west. Take 80 to Highway 95, picking that up just east of Reno, then head south. Take 95 to Vegas, and disappear. Or go to Beatty and take 374 through Death Valley, going into California. But who did that with an ancient van, a sunburn, and a kid along for the ride? If she wanted to go into California, it was better to go back north out of Hawthorne, catch up to Interstate 80 again, and go through Reno. There was no reason to go through Tonopah except to go to Vegas.

There were three very easy things to do in Vegas.

First, she could get money in Vegas. Simple theft worked best, but there were some legit ways to do it.

Second, she could get a new vehicle in Vegas. Cars were cheap there, and easy to buy with cash.

And third, she could disappear in Vegas. Thousands of people did it every year.

No one cared about transients in Vegas. No one even noticed.

If there was a good place to disappear in the western half of the United States, then Las Vegas was it.

They needed to find that woman. He wanted to catch her as soon as possible.

Before she and that little girl vanished, forever.

— 39 —

Stupid, the things that distracted one. Bastiano Dirksen was distracted by his own men on a problem they could have solved themselves. Problems with various connections, problems with people who should cooperate with Dirksen just when they heard his name, and of course they hadn't cooperated.

Then his men had checked with him: *What do you want done, Boss*? As if he had to explain it to them. He had them checked for wires, just in case, because people working for him shouldn't be that dense.

Even then, he hadn't really committed. He had waved a hand, said, "Take care of it," and let them decide what that meant. Later, if the problem was still alive, he would tell the dumb bastards to take care of it all over again, and if the problem lived after that, he would fire the dumb bastards and hire some other dumb bastards to take their place. And maybe have the second set of dumb bastards deal with the first.

He had talked to his current set of dumb bastards in the living room of his suite. When they left, he returned to his office via the bedroom where he stopped for a moment and stared at that motionless crane.

How much money had he lost in the economic meltdown? Five million? Ten? Twenty?

People like him, people whose hands were mostly in illegitimate pies, weren't supposed to lose money in a bad economy. They were supposed to make money.

But billions had disappeared on paper during that meltdown, billions in real wealth, and some of that should've come to him. That, more than anything, made him want this fifteen million dollars in cash. It probably made other people want it as well.

And because he had to deal with stupidity for nearly an hour, he had lost a bit of advantage. Now he really did have to pull in Cahill.

Dirksen sat at his mahogany desk and picked up the cell he had used to contact Cahill earlier. He hit redial, and within a minute, Cahill picked up.

"Now what?" Cahill spoke softly. So he was in the office, and he didn't want anyone to hear.

Dirksen could hear the rustle of movement. Cahill clearly was going somewhere for privacy, so no one would over hear.

"Stay at your desk," Dirksen said.

"Are you nuts?" Cahill said. "I—"

"This will only take a minute, and I need you to write this down."

Cahill sighed. The rustling repeated, along with the squeak of a chair. "What?"

"I need you to trace a license plate for me."

"There are illegal computer programs for that," Cahill snapped.

"Really?" Dirksen made the sarcasm in his voice clear. It meant: *Yes, I know, but I'm not going to acknowledge it in case this call is being recorded.*

"Really," Cahill said.

"Well, this one is unique. You'll see," Dirksen said. "Here's the number. It's a Wisconsin plate—"

And he rattled off the vowels and letters.

"—it belongs to a van," Dirksen said, "last seen outside of Storvick's house."

"How do you know that?" Cahill asked.

"I know a lot of things," Dirksen said. "Call me back with the information as soon as you have it."

"Or what?" Cahill asked.

"Or you know what," Dirksen said. "We had this conversation. In California."

"And I'm no longer in California."

"Do you think that matters to your boss?"

There was enough of a pause for Dirksen to deduce that Cahill believed his past sins would matter to his current boss. "No," Cahill lied.

"Then don't call me," Dirksen said. "But it's your choice."

And then he hung up. Cahill would call. Clearly, he wouldn't call from the Hawthorne Police Department, but he would call. And Dirksen could find the woman, and find out what she knew about the cash, and maybe he could even have his current set of stupid bastards get the information out of her.

Or maybe, if she was pretty, he would do it himself.

After all, he was getting tired of trusting others.

And waiting for that crane to move.

— 40 —

There were more boxes than Moira remembered. She'd been driving with them in the back of the van for nearly a week, and somehow she thought there were only about five. God, she must've been hyped up on adrenaline when she shoved them into the van in the first place.

She'd shot the bastard, then grabbed Kasey and made a run for it. And Kasey let out a moan as they passed the boxes in the basement. *My stuff*....

She hadn't touched the stuff after Moira got it into the van. Kasey had taken that damn Barbie and nothing else. But Moira had touched the boxes. She'd taken out clothes and underwear, much of it too small, and used it until she got to a Walmart outside of Minneapolis (or was that St. Paul? She always got those towns confused), and then she went inside with Kasey and bought an entire kid's summer wardrobe for less than fifty dollars.

Even then, she'd missed some things. She hadn't planned on Kasey being so lost. She hadn't planned on how much traveling with a kid would cost her.

She hadn't planned on that van being so rundown.

She'd gone in with a rental, left it parked at a vacant house a few blocks away, and taken Royce's van on purpose. The mattress he'd had bungeed to the roof had been a bonus.

But she had never planned to fill the back with boxes.

And she certainly hadn't planned to unload them here, now.

Goddamn that kid, making her feel all proprietary.

Goddamn that kid, for tempting her.

I don't do families, she said, and she meant it a variety of ways. She didn't normally get into the middle of them, except in cases like this when the kidnapper was actually doing something bad besides taking custody of his own kid, and she didn't kill entire families, because kids were always blameless even when they were being shitty little bastards (where'd they learn it, huh? She firmly believed all behavior was learned, and up until puberty could be changed). And she didn't belong to a family. Not a real family, which she never ever had, and not one of those cutesy TV families, made up of friends who liked and understood and went to bat for each other. Such unadulterated crap. She usually changed the channel when she came across that shit.

She lifted boxes from the van to Analyn's SUV, which was running. The air smelled of exhaust and sweat and baked asphalt. Kasey was supposed to be in the car because the air conditioner was running, but she stood outside and watched, her eyes big.

Her stuff.

She knew it was her stuff and she was going to be leaving Moira.

Analyn tried to help, but she couldn't lift the very first box. Besides, Moira didn't want her all sweaty. She wanted Analyn above reproach in case someone stopped her and questioned her.

Moira didn't know why someone would stop her and question her, but best to be prepared.

So Moira was moving the boxes herself, and dripping like a goddamn stuck pig. She had shoved them into the back end, which was really big, thank God. She had five still, and she almost suggested that they leave them, except for that look on Kasey's face.

A wail: *My stuff....*

Yeah. Her stuff. Best not to leave anything in the van that tied them to it.

Moira wiped a hand over her face and looked at Analyn and Kasey. They didn't look a lot alike at first glance, but now they did, the set of their jaws, their heads tilted at the same angle, the same look of worried fear in their eyes. In fact, now she wondered why she ever thought they were dissimilar. They were as alike as two people could be.

Moira almost told Analyn to clean out the front seat, but then she remembered her gun. Instead, she reached inside the front window herself, grabbed the Gatorade and guzzled it, immediately feeling a little better.

Almost done.

Almost done, and she'd leave them to their little domestic drama. She tossed the Gatorade into the white trash bag that Analyn magically produced from her car. What kind of woman traveled with trash bags? Not that Moira was complaining. She would make use of it, cleaning out the last of her stuff, then wiping the entire van down.

She'd been really cautious. Even the parking spot she'd chosen was hard to see. The hotel didn't have cameras (except one inside, on the desk). The businesses across the street probably did, but they couldn't see into this blind spot. The cameras might've caught the three of them walking in this direction, but they wouldn't show what happened to the three of them, particularly when Moira made Analyn drive them out of the parking lot via that back way.

Moira looked at the front seat of the SUV, near the air conditioning. Almost.

And once she got into that car, she wasn't going to say anything. Not about counseling, not about what Kasey needed, not about the things that Kasey saw.

It wasn't her business.

As soon as Analyn dropped her off, Moira would forget all about Kasey. She had to.

It was the only way she could continue.

It was the only way she knew how to survive.

— 41 —

Cahill ran the license plate himself. He went out to one of the squad cars to do it. It was easier to run plates through the traffic cop's system, designed to find anything and red flag it so a cop, who pulled someone over on a traffic violation, knew if they found an armed and dangerous escaped felon or a just housewife speeding on her way home from the mall.

It felt hotter outside. The flag above the station flapped in the wind. The wind tore the sweat off him before it could even form. Sometimes he missed that sweat. He was hot before he even knew how he'd gotten that way.

He sat half in and half out of the squad, feeing a heat headache build between his eyes. Or maybe it was a Dirksen headache.

This was starting all over again. That bastard was working his way back into Cahill's life. First it would be updates on the investigation, then favors like this one, then something big, something that would compromise him here—maybe the death of someone like Storvick (*C'mon Cahill, they're just vermin anyway*) or moving a bit of cash (meaning wads of it) from one part of Nevada to another or looking the other way when one of Dirksen's thugs got arrested.

Cahill's hands were shaking as he punched in the plate—not because he was frightened. He wasn't. He was angry. He thought he had gotten

170

away from all of this. He had moved to the ass-end of nowhere, a place where he figured his legitimate skills would get him a job, and his illegitimate skills had no value at all.

And somehow Dirksen found a way to hook him, to get him to do the dirty work.

At least Cahill had gotten something out of it. He had added the license plate number to the original APB he'd sent out on the van, and he had targeted the Las Vegas area. After he ran this license plate, and had the woman's name and image, he would add that too.

The small computer screen in front of the dash gave him a recent red flag, posted late last night: The van was stolen.

That surprised him. The woman, with her sunburn and her child, looked like she fit in that rusted-out, ancient van. And, in fact, why would someone steal an ancient van—and keep it? If you had the skills to steal a car, why not replace that car somewhere along I-80? Take an SUV that would hide the child or at least have tinted windows to protect from the sun.

The red flag didn't stop with the theft. The flag had the highest possible warning. The van was stolen from a murder scene. The van's owner, Royce Gallagher, was found dead in his basement yesterday, his van and some of his possessions missing.

Contact information ran along the top and bottom of the screen. The detectives involved in the Gallagher case put a high priority on the van, and anyone spotting it had to report it.

That was the alert, which was why Dirksen's illegal program couldn't get in. Cahill's inquiry had already been captured by the FBI and the Wisconsin state police. If he didn't call them, someone from one of those agencies would call him.

He picked up his cell, started to dial, and then stopped. If Dirksen had tried to breach this information with an illegal program, then they might have record of the attempted hack. If their system was as poor as Nevada's, they wouldn't know anything other than an attempt had been made.

If the system was as good as California's, they'd know who made the contact. But knowing Dirksen, he would have made that contact through some kind of firewall.

But Cahill had a way around the firewall.

He grinned to himself, glanced at the recent calls on his cell, and pulled Dirksen's number. He wrote the number on the ticket tablet in the front seat.

Then he dialed the "contact immediately" number on the car's computer screen.

He was going to enjoy this call. It would put some control back into his life.

And it might ruin Dirksen, once and for all.

— 42 —

Quiznos or Subway. Sometimes it seemed like her entire life was defined by those two choices.

Officer Leslie Foster sat in a parking lot near one of Vegas's many strip malls, trying to choose which sandwich she would have for her meal break. She couldn't call this meal *lunch*, even though it was her lunch, because it fell closer to everyone else's dinner.

And like most traffic cops, she ate poorly—fast food made quickly— but she really did want to watch her girlish figure. She didn't want to have what she privately called McDonald's belly—that round jiggle of fat under a crisply starched blue shirt, a jiggle that said she wasn't in shape, hadn't been in shape for years, and would never be in shape again.

Subway. Whenever she thought of fat, she thought of that Jared kid, even though they'd stopped the commercials with him holding up pants the size of a house, claiming that between exercise and Subway, he'd worked it all off.

She could do that too, if she didn't get the cookie and the potato chips. But the cookie and potato chips were the real reason she ate there.

She put the squad into drive, moved across the parking lot without her seatbelt on (*Quick! Someone arrest that woman!*) and stopped in front of Subway. Quiznos was across the street. She was committed now.

Just as she put the car into park, a revised APB came across her screen. The APB targeted the Vegas area. She sighed, wanting her break, as well as a regular Coke, those chips, and that damn cookie.

But she was a good cop and watched the information scroll.

Sunburned woman, child, van with Wisconsin plate, stolen from a murder scene, child could be in danger. Act immediately.

"Son of a bitch," she said, and tugged on her seatbelt, sandwich forgotten. She knew roughly where that woman was. If she hurried back to Boulder Highway, she'd probably see the van.

She put the squad in reverse, backed up—narrowly missing another car in the lot, then shifted back to drive and peeled out—no sirens, no lights. She didn't call for backup either, and wouldn't until she had the van in her sights.

But she did contact the dispatch, reporting that she had seen the van about thirty minutes before, and she had an idea where it was. She promised to radio in if she found anything.

Damn. She felt like an idiot. Her gut had told her that something was wrong. She'd seen that mattress half-falling off the van, saw the woman's wary look, and listened to the half-baked excuse:

It—the—I—this is my boyfriend's van. He loaned it to me to get here. I've got a job at the Mirage, my old boss hired me back, but I couldn't get here with my stuff, so he loaned us the van, and he's flying in this weekend to get it and drive it back, you can call him if you want....

Foster hadn't believed it, not then, because the woman's voice had been nervous but her eyes hadn't. So she asked the kid. The kid, who said she was happy to come home to Vegas, who said she'd been born here.

The kid, who didn't seem like she'd been coached.

Foster had trusted the kid and the kid had let her down.

Foster's cheeks warmed. She'd even helped that woman put the mattress back on top of the van. And she'd told her to put something on that sunburn.

The woman must've laughed as Foster drove off. That burned more than anything.

The woman had played her for a fool.

Well, if she hadn't lied, if she truly was meeting someone at the motels on the Boulder Highway, then the van shouldn't be hard to spot, even if she took the damn mattress off.

It would take Foster ten minutes to get there, another five to look around.

And another five or ten for backup.

But Foster didn't want to think about that. Besides, she could take a woman that tiny. Anyone could.

It was for moments like this that she kept herself in shape.

She made her way through the traffic, heading to Boulder Highway, praying that she wouldn't arrive too late.

— 43 —

The last damn box. Of course it was heavy. Of course it didn't quite fit into the SUV. With Kasey and her booster taking up half of the back seat, the only place for the last box was the passenger side floor of the front seat.

Which meant that Moira couldn't get into the car. Not without sitting really uncomfortably.

She stood for one long moment, staring at that floor space, then at Kasey's face.

My stuff…

Moira didn't want to hear that wail again, and she didn't want to repack the damn box or the damn car.

Analyn had moved some kind of garbage container specially designed for SUVs so that Moira could put the box in the front seat. Analyn had no idea that Moira had planned to leave with them.

So the change of plans would be Moira's own, and no one else had to know.

She tried to wedge the box on the floor, but the box didn't fit. Instead she put it on that leather seat, the one that had looked so inviting just a moment ago.

"That's it," she said, wiping her hands on her shirt.

Analyn nodded, hovered, uncertain. Of course. She wasn't the kind of woman used to finishing this kind of transaction.

And Kasey hovered, too, closer to Moira than to Analyn.

Moira put her hand on Kasey's back, propelled her forward just a little, like she would do when they were on the highway together, after a Happy Meal and a chocolate shake.

"Better get in the car, hon," Moira said, her voice softer than she had intended.

Kasey shook her head.

Moira sighed. She didn't want to finish this up with Kasey outside. But the kid wasn't going to budge. Moira glanced at Analyn, who looked out of her damn depth. That bothered Moira more than anything. The woman had clearly been expecting the pre-trauma Kasey, and the pre-trauma Kasey was gone forever.

Moira crouched. "You remember that phone number?" she asked.

"Yeah," Kasey whispered.

Moira had given her the number in case they got separated, in case Moira got arrested or killed. The number of Dealmakers, the company Moira more or less worked for, none of it legit, but all of it goody two-shoes—if you could call kidnapping and the occasional murder goody two-shoes. Only bad people died, she would've told Kasey if Kasey had asked. Maybe the pre-trauma Kasey would've asked, but this one didn't.

This one had already learned that too many questions could get you in trouble.

"Tell me the number," Moira said.

Kasey did. She recited it like Moira had taught her, to the ABC melody, and it had stuck in her brain.

Analyn was watching, clearly fascinated.

"If something goes wrong," Moira said. "Really, really bad, like what happened before with your dad and the babysitter, you call that number. Okay?"

"It won't go bad," Analyn said.

But Moira ignored her, looking at Kasey.

"What if I don't like it?" Kasey whispered.

"Don't like what?" Moira asked.

"Home." Kasey's voice shook.

"You won't at first," Moira said. "It'll be different. But it'll be okay. You call me only if something happens like before. Or if someone wants to put you into the system. You remember what I said about the system?"

"Never let anyone put you in the system," Kasey said, full voice.

"My God," Analyn said.

"I mean it." Moira looked up at Analyn, speaking to her now. "You fuck up and Child Services shows up, this kid will call me. And I'll deal with you."

Analyn paled, her eyes wide. "I won't f—screw up. I won't."

"Good," Moira said.

She hugged Kasey before she even realized what she was doing. Suddenly her arms were around the kid who smelled of child sweat and was hotter than she should be, her bones poking against her T-shirt.

Then Moira pulled back. "You were great," she said. "Best partner I ever had."

Kasey grinned. Her very first happy expression. Just as they were going to part.

"Now," Moira said. "Get in the car."

Kasey nodded. She started for the back door, stopped, and kissed Moira on the cheek. Then she ran to the car and climbed in.

Analyn watched. Moira stayed crouched for a moment, the feel of Kasey's dry lips on her skin.

She hadn't lied to that kid. If she heard Kasey got into the system, she'd come back here and fucking kill Analyn.

Because that kid had been the best. The best ever.

And Moira was letting her go.

She stood.

"Everything in my account?" Moira asked.

Analyn nodded. "Transferred, while you were moving boxes."

Moira had seen her on the phone. She'd better be right. The money had better be in the account.

"Cash," Moira said, holding out her hand.

Analyn nodded nervously. She reached into her purse and pulled out an envelope with the logo of *New York New York* on it. Moira took the envelope and counted the money. It was all there.

"The phone," Moira said.

She wanted the phone Analyn had used during the entire week. Moira had e-mailed photos to that phone from various computers all along I-80, computers that would suffer their own investigations soon, if they weren't being investigated already.

Analyn handed over an iPhone. Spendy for a bolt phone, and sadly, Moira would have to destroy it.

"The key to your room," Moira said, holding out her hand again.

"What?" Analyn asked.

"Your room here," Moira said. "I want the key."

"Why?" Analyn asked.

Moira sighed. "I'm not going to trash it. I need a shower before I hit the road again. You already paid for the room, it's not under your name, and you're not staying. So give me the key."

"Oh, sorry." Analyn handed it to her. An old-fashioned key with an old-fashioned plastic ring that had the room number on it, just in case Moira forgot.

"You be good to that kid," Moira said.

"I will," Analyn said, but kept hovering. Moira was tempted to put her hand on Analyn's back and push her toward the car, just like she always did with Kasey.

Instead, Moira said. "Now get the hell out of here and forget that this ever happened."

"You're not going to tell me what exactly happened to Royce?"

"No," Moira said. "And neither is Kasey. Maybe she can tell a therapist, but not you. You need deniability."

"What?"

"Think it through," Moira said. "As you drive out of here."

Analyn nodded, a bit shell-shocked, just like the others Moira had dealt with when she worked for Dealmakers. People out of their depth. People on the edges of the law for the first and only time.

People who needed people like her just once, and wanted to forget her.

Moira turned her back on Analyn, on the car, on Kasey. She wanted to wave good-bye, but she didn't. She just walked across the parking lot, past the camera, head up, going to the room.

Behind her, she heard the SUV start. The engine purred, unlike that rattle-trap van. The SUV drove past her, Kasey in the back seat, her face pressed against the window.

Looking engaged for the first time.

Looking sad.

Looking scared.

Moira waved after all.

And Kasey waved back.

— 44 —

Cahill sat half in and half out of the squad car, staring at the alert. The squad was running, the air conditioning on. He should've gotten out and walked back into the police department, but he didn't. This was his case, his idea, his *lie,* and he wanted to keep it all to himself.

His cell phone was pressed against his ear. He'd gone through two detectives to the guy who was in charge of the Wisconsin police investigation. That guy had put him on speaker in some hollow meeting room. They actually had a goddamn task force, with ties to the FBI Sex Crimes unit. Everyone had introduced themselves with name and rank.

Like he cared.

The guy in charge—a man by the name of Pedersen—had given him the lowdown.

Royce Gallagher had been found yesterday, murdered in his basement. He lived in a nice neighborhood and someone complained about a faint fetid smell between their buildings. That someone actually called animal control first, thinking that some kind of creature had died on the property, and figured that Royce Gallagher was out of town, since they hadn't seen his van for a few days.

Instead, Royce Gallagher was dead in the basement, shot twice with a .38, blood and brains all over his secret room, a room designed to look like a little girl's bedroom.

181

A room with still and video cameras and a one-way mirror so that someone could watch whoever had lived inside.

Royce Gallagher had made a series of child porn films, the latest with a little blond girl, "cute as a button," Pedersen had said sadly.

That little blond girl sounded like a ringer for the kid traveling with the woman in the van.

"You got pictures of the kid?" Cahill asked, then realized how that sounded. "Head shots, clean stuff."

"Yeah. We can send them," Pedersen said. "You think she's the kid you saw?"

"I didn't see her," Cahill said. "But a number of witnesses described her. And I'd like to show the picture around."

"You got it," Pedersen said.

"Awful quick to put a task force together," Cahill said.

There was a pause. Then Pedersen said, "It initially had to do with child abductions."

Cahill let that sink in for a moment, then decided he didn't want to think about it. "With all the cameras and video equipment in the room, does that mean you got a recording of the murder?"

"Sadly, no," Pedersen said. "Someone took the disk with that image on it."

"The someone who killed him," Cahill said.

"We assume so," Pedersen said.

"Just like you assume that someone took the van."

"It was last seen leaving the neighborhood the day that Gallagher died."

"With a woman and a little girl in it?"

"We don't know," Pedersen said. "Right now, she's just a person of interest."

"In three other homicides," Cahill said. He didn't mention Tonopah. He figured that wasn't in the pattern, an accidental kill, a surprise kill. They didn't need to know.

Yet.

"Three?"

"Two pedophiles and a rapist," Cahill said. "Sound familiar?"

"Jesus," someone else said. "You think we have a serial killer?"

"I thought we had a spree killer," Cahill said. "But now I'm hearing about connections. You guys are the task force. You should see if these people did business together."

They buzzed on the other end, conversations too soft for him to catch more than a word here or there.

"I do have a question, though," Cahill said. "How come you guys never issued an AMBER?"

"An AMBER Alert?" Pedersen asked.

"Yeah, on the kid and the van," Cahill said.

There was a long silence. The heat had crept into the squad, made his face hot.

"Because," Pedersen said. "We didn't know she was in the van. We still don't."

"You should've had cops in every state looking for that kid," Cahill said.

"The videos weren't time-stamped," someone else said. He sounded official. Cahill wasn't good with voices, but he would wager that this guy was the FBI liaison, the real person in charge. "We don't know when they were made."

There was something else in his tone, something flat and ugly and unsaid.

"You thought she was dead," Cahill said. As hot as he had been a moment before, he felt a chill now. "You *believed* she was dead."

"Detective—" said the Official Voice.

"How many dead children did you find in that basement?" Cahill asked.

"In the basement?" Pedersen asked as the Official Voice said, "None."

"Where did you find them?" Cahill asked.

"We haven't released any of this," Official Voice said. "We're going over records now. This'll be ugly when it breaks."

"You thought it was contained," Cahill said. "He was dead, the kids were dead. You have a list of his subscribers, end of story. How hard were you going to look for the killer?"

Official Voice, bristling. "We've been looking very hard."

"We thought the killer was someone in the group, someone Gallagher knew."

"You didn't think it was a little blond vigilante, did you?" Cahill said. "You missed it all. Or maybe you didn't. Sounds like she's cleaning up some messes for you."

Again, silence. Then Official Voice said, "We never heard of her until now."

"Well, you have her," Cahill said. "License plate, the van's heading to Vegas. I'm sure you got an FBI office there that can handle her, right?"

"Why do you want her?" Official Voice said. "Who'd she kill?"

"Two people today," Cahill said. "Doesn't sound like the right environment for a kid, now does it?"

"Shit," Official Voice said loud enough for Cahill to hear. "We'll get on it. Send us what you have."

And then the conference call ended. Silence. No breathing, no rustling, no nothing.

Not even a thank-you.

Fucking FBI. And he hadn't told them about Dirksen yet.

He almost let it go, but didn't dare. He was about to pull the phone away from his ear, hit redial, when Pedersen came on the line.

"Sorry I had to put you on hold," he said, and from the sound of his voice he had moved elsewhere. "They're really pissed off. We've been behind this one from the beginning."

"No shit," Cahill said.

"We appreciate your call," Pedersen said.

"Or at least you do," Cahill said.

"Or at least I do." There was a smile in Pedersen's voice.

"I got one more piece of information," Cahill said. "There's a hit in our system on this license number."

"A hit?" Pedersen asked.

"Someone tried to hack in and trace the plate with an illegal download program. It was on a cell. We capture numbers that do that. You want it?"

"Hell, yes," Pedersen said.

"Don't know if it means anything," Cahill said, the lie feeling really, really good.

"We'll take it anyway," Pedersen said.

So Cahill gave him Dirksen's cell phone number. Which would give them a GPS signal, one they could easily track with the FBI involved.

He and Pedersen exchanged pleasantries, and then the call really and truly ended.

Cahill shut off his phone and stuck it in his pocket.

"Take that you goddamn cocksucker," he said softly, imagining Dirksen's round face. "Take that."

— 45 —

The shower felt good. Cool water, spraying on her sunburn, wiping off the road dirt, the grit, the little spray of blood.

And any gun residue—at least, she hoped.

She lathered the cheap little bar of hotel soap and used it to wash her hair, her face, her entire body. She couldn't remember the last time a shower felt this good—even though she was in an ancient shower stall and the water pipes squealed.

She wanted to stay in the shower for the rest of her life, but she didn't dare. She had to get out of here. The shower was only an intermediary step toward getting away.

She had already wiped down the van, getting as much of it as possible. She knew that she had prints everywhere, but she wanted to make sure any possible blood trace was gone.

More importantly, she wanted all traces of Kasey out of that van. The kid had been listed in the Missing Children's database, which meant her fingerprints were in the system—her DNA, too, probably. Moira didn't want anyone to be able to prove that Kasey had been the kid in the van.

Moira left the registration in the glove box, but got her own kit out of there. She always traveled light. She'd even taken one of Analyn's garbage bags. Moira put the identification she'd given to the cop in that bag, as well as the clothes she had on today, along with the shoes she'd worn when she shot that guy in Tonopah, and the flip-flops she'd worn ever since.

That left her with her boots, but it didn't matter. Flip-flops were easy to buy. Besides, she could afford sandals now. Good high quality sandals.

She got out of the shower and wrapped one thin terrycloth towel around her hair. She used the other towel to wipe off as best she could. The thing wasn't very absorbent.

She wiped aloe all over her skin, hoping that would tone down the sunburn a bit. She also needed some hair dye. She wasn't sure if she should go black or auburn or green.

Probably not green. She didn't want to call too much attention to herself.

Besides, she didn't have tattoos or piercings to go with the wacky hair.

She tossed the towel in the shower. Then she got dressed, wearing clothes she hadn't worn since Wisconsin. Her getaway clothes.

She'd planned for this, but not for the extreme heat. At least the blouse was cotton and soft, the jeans old and well loved.

The boots were the problem. She slid them on, wincing when her feet hit the hard lifts inside. Boots with a heel plus the lift would make her walk different. They would also make people guess she was a few inches taller than she was.

If she did this right—and went out with her hair wet—no one would suspect she was the same woman who drove the van.

At least, not at first glance.

Then she could catch the bus downtown.

This was the tough part. She'd hoped Analyn could drop her downtown, but that wasn't going to happen.

Besides, it probably kept the kid clear.

But Moira had to look inconspicuous as she walked, look like she belonged, look normal.

And here in Vegas, where no one walked in the heat, that would be damn hard.

But she had to try.

And she had to succeed.

— 46 —

Foster found the van at the third motel she tried. She would've missed it, but after cruising past the first two motels, she decided to drive through the parking lot.

There, to one side, near a copse of spindly things some long-ago architect had thought of as trees, was the van, listing a little to one side. The mattress was sliding again. It still had only two bungee cords hooking it to the top.

She parked directly behind the van and radioed it in. She was a good little traffic cop, making sure that she included the fact that it was in the APB and tied to a possible murder.

"I will proceed with caution," she said, although she wasn't entirely sure why. The woman she'd encountered before hadn't looked so tough. The little girl had looked downright scared.

Besides, the van was empty. It had been parked long enough that dust had accumulated from the day's wind.

Even if Foster hadn't seen the dust, she would've known it was empty. No one sat in a van like that without the motor running. Not in this heat. Not even with the windows down.

Still, she checked her weapon before she got out of the squad. She left the squad running. She walked to the van's driver's side, and confirmed her suspicions.

No one sat inside the van.

She peered down.

No one crouched on the floor, here or in the back seat.

In fact, the kid's booster seat was gone.

So were the boxes.

Just the mattress remained.

Foster frowned. That was weird. Why take the boxes but leave a mattress you'd driven with some difficulty all the way from Wisconsin? So that she looked like she was moving?

That had been the assumption that Foster had made.

That had probably been the assumption everyone had made.

Or maybe the answer was simple: maybe the woman had a friend, like she claimed, only they decided not to drive the van to the friend's house. They'd loaded the boxes into the friend's truck, and driven away.

Which would explain why the booster seat was missing.

Still, Foster walked around the van, cautiously making certain no one was in the very back.

The thing was empty. Extremely empty. No litter, no toys, no water bottles, nothing.

Like it had been left.

All except for the mattress.

She slipped on a glove, then tried the passenger door.

It opened. The van was unlocked.

So she looked inside, remembering the plain sight rule. Then, on a whim, she whacked the glove box, and it tumbled open.

There was the registration, the one she had seen, with the dead guy's name across it.

… he loaned us the van, and he's flying in this weekend to get it and drive it back, you can call him if you want….

Yeah, right. That woman was smart. She knew no one would call the bastard, not with that mattress on the roof. Besides, who stole an ancient van, stuffed it full of boxes and a kid, tied a mattress to the roof, and used it as a getaway car?

Either someone very naïve or someone very smart.

Or maybe he had loaned her the van, and she had no idea he was dead.

Not that it was Foster's call. She peered inside the glove box, saw nothing else, and gently eased it closed. No sense in leaving it open. Let someone else pound on it and get the same information.

She backed out, closed the door, and sighed.

The woman was gone. So was the little girl.

Then Foster looked at the motel.

Unless they'd unloaded and gone inside.

Foster wouldn't have unloaded those boxes in the heat. If nothing else, she would've waited until full dark, especially with a sunburn like that woman had. But Foster wasn't an expert in how other people thought.

Besides, no backup had gotten here yet.

All she had to do was check with the desk clerk. A tiny sunburned blond woman and a matching kid would be hard to miss, particularly if they showed up in that van.

Foster shut off the squad and headed to the front door of the hotel. It would be nice if she could resolve this all on her own.

She could use the points. She didn't want to be a traffic cop forever.

Maybe someday, she could be a detective.

Maybe someday, she could be someone important.

If she caught enough lucky breaks.

— 47 —

Red and blue lights reflected on the white curtain pulled over the window. Moira cursed. The cops were here.

She made herself take a deep breath. This wasn't the best part of Vegas. Just because there were police lights didn't mean the cops were there for her.

She could be overreacting.

She walked to the window, grabbed the edge of the curtain, and pulled it back slightly. The police car was sitting at the far end of the lot, its lights on, but its door closed.

It had parked in several cars—including the van.

She cursed again, nonsense words under her breath, like she had done the entire time she traveled with Kasey. A new habit, one she could shed now that Kasey was gone.

If a cop had the van parked in, that couldn't be a coincidence. Moira leaned against the wall, trying to see as much of the parking lot as she could. She couldn't see the cops who belonged to that car.

She hurried to the bathroom and opened the window there just a crack. No other police cars in the lot.

Yet.

She took a deep breath. So far as she knew, no one was looking for her. If someone had been looking for her, the traffic cop who helped with the mattress would've taken her in.

Moira was ready to leave here anyway. No sense dallying. She would just avoid the cop car.

She took her purse and slung it over her shoulder. Then she hefted the garbage bag.

The Dumpster was around back. She just needed to look like a hotel guest who was tidying up her own trash.

(How many hotel guests did that? Not many, she supposed. But what the hell. She had no other choice.)

She kept the key, tucking it in the front pocket of her jeans. Then she went back to the main window and peered out.

She didn't see anyone in the lot. No cops in uniform, no other guests.

So she sidled over to the door and quietly pulled it open. The heat made her sunburn ache. Dammit. She hadn't put enough lotion on after all.

But she didn't even try to fix that.

Instead, she let herself out, quietly closing the door behind her, holding it so that it didn't even snick as the latch engaged.

Then she kept her head up and walked to the side of the building, her heart pounding. As she rounded the corner, she moved her eyes just a little.

A cop was heading to the front door of the motel, where Moira had gone in. Where the front desk was. Where Moira had stood hand-in-hand with Kasey and asked for Analyn.

The damn desk clerk had given her the room number by memory.

Moira's heart pounded.

She risked a glance at the cop.

It was that damn woman cop, the one who had helped with the mattress.

Moira caught her breath. Fuck. That meant the cop was there for her, and there was some kind of bulletin.

Someone had tied her to the Tonopah shooting. Or the Hawthorne shooting.

Or some damn thing.

Moira walked as quickly as she could around the building, and tossed the white bag into the Dumpster. Then she continued across the parking lot. Ahead, there were more hotels, a few convenience stores, and a used car lot.

For a moment she was tempted. She just had to get into that lot, buy a car, and get the hell out of here.

But she made herself take a deep breath. No car lots. No change of plans.

Instead she headed to the bus stop on the corner. Two women waited there already, both in uniform. Maids, probably getting off shift from a nearby hotel.

One was in uniform, but the other wasn't. They were both taller than Moira.

She nodded at them. "When's the next bus due?" she asked.

"Where?" One of the women asked. She was missing her front tooth.

Moira wanted to say, "Anywhere," but she refrained. Seeming panicked was the wrong thing to do.

"The Strip," Moira said.

The woman opened her hands slightly. "Dunno."

"The next bus ends at the Downtown Transportation Center," the other woman said.

"Near Fremont Street?" Moira asked.

"I thought you were going to the Strip," the woman said.

Moira shrugged.

"You can transfer," the first woman said. "But you can gamble anywhere, you know. You don't have to go to the Strip or downtown. There's a casino not far from here."

"It's okay," Moira said. "I'm not interested in local casinos. I want to pluck some tourists."

Both women laughed. "Plucking tourists" was a phrase usually used by poker players for taking the money of strangers. Moira had just set herself up as a regular player, maybe even someone who made her living off cards.

"Pluck a few for me," said the first woman.

A bus rounded the corner. Moira turned toward it, not just so that she could see it better, but also because it gave her a good view of the motel.

So far, no one had followed her.

So far, she was safe.

"That bus stopping here?" she asked.

"Yes," the first woman said. "That's our bus."

Their bus. It felt like their bus. Like her bus. As the bus slowed, she saw two more cop cars turn into the motel's parking lot.

Then the bus obstructed her vision. The women got on, even though she wanted to shove them out of the way.

She followed, took a seat in the middle, checked for the emergency brake, and clutched her purse to her chest.

Almost there.

Just a few more hours—and just a little more luck.

— 48 —

Cahill hadn't called back.

Dirksen stood in his office, hands in his back pockets like a working stiff, staring out the window. The view from his office showed the strip only, no crane. At night, the lights from the various hotels lit the office as if it were still daylight.

He thought that view was beautiful.

But, during the day, the view of the Strip showed it at its worst. Hotels and casinos bracketed by junk—weird garish stores that only catered to tourists. A road much too wide, filled with too many cars. Smog hiding the mountains, making the sunlight gray.

He could dim the windows, but he did not.

Instead, he thought.

Cahill hadn't called back.

Perhaps that license plate was proving more difficult than he expected.

Perhaps the man was no longer afraid of him.

Dirksen had spoken to the team in Hawthorne. Davis hadn't come back. No one had heard from him at all. Lyman was back, but he had seen nothing. And the kid was still at the house, watching the street, hoping that someone would show up for the meet with Storvick.

But Dirksen knew no one would show up. He had already sent Lyman to keep an eye on Storvick's wife, but he knew that would do no good either. If Storvick had told the wife what he was into, she would have already told the police. Or gone somewhere other than the fleabag hotel where she was spending the night.

Dirksen had seen the videos. If she had known what Storvick was doing, she would have been frightened as well as upset. Terrified, actually. And she wasn't that kind of terrified. She was the kind of terrified people got when someone else broke into their homes, not the kind of terrified people got when they were hiding something.

The woman in the Wisconsin van was Dirksen's only hope.

He needed Cahill.

In fact, he probably needed Cahill more than Cahill needed him.

Really, did some small-town chief of police care that his big-city detective had been on the take? Cahill had probably come clean when he moved to Hawthorne—or had come as clean as he needed to. The chief of police had probably asked why Cahill had come, and Cahill had given some song and dance about needing to get away from the corruption.

Any man with a brain would know that the corruption tainted everyone.

Of course, escaping corruption in Nevada was tricky.

But Dirksen hadn't bribed anyone in Hawthorne. So far as he knew, that town was incorruptible. The military saw to that. There was too much at stake there.

Maybe he had made a mistake threatening Cahill.

Then Dirksen shook his head. Cahill was a coward. He wouldn't've done the smart thing. He would call.

It was probably taking him time to deal with the license plate. There was some reason it had been flagged.

A commotion echoed from the front of the suite. Voices, raised voices, someone barking orders.

Dirksen looked at the door to his office and sighed.

He had men out there, of course. He would be foolish not to. But sometimes those men were more trouble than they were worth. They always want to *do* something, and guarding him didn't require much.

Mostly he guarded them, and prevented them from antagonizing the hotel too much.

So he was already irritated when he pulled his office door open.

He stepped into the living room and stopped.

Four men in black suits blocked the door.

His men were standing.

"Mr. Dirksen?" the shortest man said. He was also the oldest, his black hair threaded with silver.

Dirksen said nothing, neither confirming or denying.

The short man pulled a badge out of his suit pocket. "FBI. We need you to come with us, sir."

Dirksen stared at him. "What's this about?"

"Your attempts at hacking a Nevada police database," the FBI agent said. "You also attempted to hack into an FBI database. That's a federal offense."

Dirksen had dealt with law enforcement long enough to know better than to say anything. But normally he was prepared for the charges. He wasn't prepared for this one.

So he permitted himself one small comment. "Hacking? I'm a businessman. I don't know enough about computers to hack anything."

"You used a special program to access a license plate. That's illegal, Mr. Dirksen." The agent was still holding his badge, looking like a doofus, but the men behind him had moved their suit coats back, exposing their weapons.

These men were serious.

Then Dirksen let out a breath. No wonder Cahill hadn't called. Something major had happened. Something that involved the very plate Dirksen wanted to get.

FBI only got involved in terrorism these days, didn't it?

He let out a small breath.

If this was terrorism, then he was in deep trouble. They could lock him up and not tell anyone where he was.

"If you don't mind," Dirksen said, "we'll stay here until my lawyer arrives."

The lawyer he hadn't even called yet.

"We mind," the short man said. "Your lawyer can meet us at FBI headquarters."

"Still," Dirksen said, "since I'm not under arrest, I prefer to wait here."

"Oh, I didn't say that, sir," the agent said. "You are under arrest. And personally, I hope to hell someone throws away the key."

Dirksen looked at him with sudden interest.

"Do we know each other?" he asked.

"I know of you, Mr. Dirksen," the agent said. "Everyone does. We always thought you were bulletproof."

The agent put his badge away and pulled out handcuffs. He was smiling.

"Thank God," he said, "we were wrong."

— 49 —

Moira set her purse on the seat beside her. She no longer smelled like soap. Now she smelled like diesel. Switching buses at the Downtown Transportation Center had been harder than she thought. Vegas didn't have great public transportation. Buses operated on a whim and a prayer.

She had thought of taking a cab, but that would call attention to her. And she wanted to be invisible.

She felt very visible at the moment. The dry desert air had sucked the moisture from her hair. She looked blond and sunburned again. But she couldn't look nervous. If she did, people would notice.

Instead, she hogged the seat next to her on the bus like a local would, and gutted out the ride. She needed to get to McCarran Airport. She'd initially thought of going to the Strip or to Fremont Street and getting a cab from either location. Then no one would've noticed her, no one would've thought of her.

But she couldn't exactly do that now. And a bus did go directly to McCarran. She'd have to walk a little from the bus stop to get to long-term parking, but she could do that. And somehow she had to avoid the airport's security cameras.

A strand of hair fell in her face. Damn that. She didn't have time to do a proper disguise. She supposed she could take an extra day, dye her hair, upgrade her clothes and makeup. After all, she had the cash for it—and that was what she had initially planned to use the cash for.

But she couldn't do that now.

Not with a cop car showing up at the motel.

She almost got herself a cap near the bus terminal, but changed her mind. In this heat, a cap would look conspicuous. Instead, she would keep her face averted, and walk with purpose wherever she went. She needed to look like she belonged.

That would get her through all kinds of screening. She just had to remember everything she had learned over all the years on her own.

She was a magician, forcing people to look at her open hand when really they should have asked what she had palmed in her other hand. She was improvising, but she could do that.

She had improvised all day long, and so far it had worked.

Except for the cop car.

But she couldn't think about that.

She was only a few miles from her destination. Once she had the car, she was almost there.

She needed to concentrate on where she was going, not where she came from.

The story of her life: focus forward, because the past was too ugly to contemplate.

She settled in her seat and stared at the front of the bus. Neon glared off the windshield, blocking most of her view, but it didn't matter. The future was in front of her, and that was all she needed to know.

— 50 —

The motel room smelled of soap. The air was humid, moisture trapped in the poorly ventilated space.

Foster stood near the bathroom sink. No hair, no obvious fibers, although there would be DNA on the towels, not that it mattered. No one would do any forensic work on this room, because there was no reason to.

The blond woman had been here and now she was gone.

So was the kid.

And so was the woman she had come to meet.

The garbage cans held only the soap wrapper. The edge of the bed was slightly mussed as if someone had sat on it. The curtains were closed.

Otherwise, the motel room looked like all the other motel rooms here.

Empty.

Dammit.

The woman had clearly left, but no one had seen her go. Foster had already checked with the clerk. She didn't recognize the name on the registration, but that didn't mean anything. Besides, it was the companion whose name was registered there. Another woman, more upscale, expensive clothes, an expensive purse, an SUV.

Foster already had the guy check the security video. The blond woman was on it, but her face was hidden. The little girl was on it as well, but no visuals of her face either.

The woman who registered was a brunette, taller, and clearly nervous. She paid in cash.

The security video caught the SUV driving across the parking lot twice, once going toward the van, and once leaving the lot. But neither time did it catch the license plate numbers.

The blond woman had parked the van perfectly, so that the cameras couldn't get any information.

That wispy copse of trees prevented other security cameras in the area from getting anything as well, although the detectives would try.

There were detectives on this case now, detectives who wouldn't ask Foster what she thought, detectives who were already conducting interviews. Detectives who had given up on this room with a single glance.

Now she was giving up on it too.

She had found the van and the woman and a child. Involved in a murder—or maybe several murders.

But the woman had gotten away, and Foster didn't know how.

She had a hunch the detectives wouldn't find anything. This woman, this blond woman, had deliberately led Foster here. The van was purposefully memorable. The blond woman had done some misdirection, for what reason, Foster didn't know.

But Foster would learn from this. Next time she had an iffy traffic stop, she'd trust her gut. She'd ask a few more questions, maybe follow the car a little ways, maybe even figure out how to take some action.

Because if she had done that when she pulled the blond woman over the first time, they'd have a murderer. And they might have saved a little girl.

Or at least they would know what had really happened.

Because the one thing that Foster did know was this: that little blond girl didn't need saving. Foster had given her a chance to save herself, and that kid had been cheerful. She had said she was from Vegas and had even listed the hospital she was born in.

The blond woman had looked surprised at that. So the kid hadn't been coached.

The kid had been protecting the woman—and victims didn't do that. Not voluntarily. Especially not young kid victims. Kids were unpredictable. This kid could've said something wrong—in fact, the blond woman had clearly expected it.

But the kid hadn't said anything wrong.

And that meant something.

Foster chose to believe it meant that the kid was okay.

But as she stood in the motel room, looking at the steam fading off the mirror, she wondered.

If the blond woman had put the mattress on the van to mislead people, what had she been doing with the kid?

And why?

— 51 —

The car was exactly where she had left it. Far corner of the long-term lot, near the back, away from any cameras. Cameras caught everything in this town, but not always at the best angle.

Moira kept her head down as she walked, purse in front of her like some stooge tourist, pretending to look for her keys.

Actually, she'd been holding her keys since the last few blocks on that bus. She had a moment of panic that she had forgotten them somewhere in Nebraska or one of those many hotel rooms with Kasey.

But Moira hadn't forgotten them, although her heart had skipped a beat when the first keys she found had been Gary's. She had almost forgotten she'd stolen them.

The car was covered in dust. A blue sedan, two years old. Because studies said that most women her age drove minivans—the modern kind—or SUVs or family-sized sedans. SUVs guzzled gas. Minivans were designed for carrying cargo and kids and stuff. Moira didn't want something that was designed for carrying stuff.

She wanted something people thought of as here-to-there cars, com-mute cars, cars you did not use for hauling. She chose the sedan and bought it with the last of her previous job's cash, then parked it here just after she'd gotten the assignment to work for Analyn.

It had all come together perfectly.

She walked around the sedan. Tires were still inflated. No one had dented it with a door and left a note.

Everything seemed just fine.

She clicked her remote and the trunk popped open. She leaned into it, back to the camera, and set the larger purse inside. She took a smaller purse out of the back, and slung it over her shoulder.

Now she looked like an efficient traveler, if she showed up on any of the cameras at all. If she did, she'd be at the edge of the screen, not the focus.

She checked the license plate. Still covered with mud and dirt, just like the undercarriage of the car. That stuff had been fresh when she parked here—she'd ladled it on herself—but it was weeks old now. It would fall off as she drove.

She could only hope it would hold until she got out of the lot.

But she had no control over that part. Just like she hadn't had control over much of this day.

Her heart was pounding and her mouth was dry. She resisted the urge to look in the direction of the nearest camera.

Instead, she walked to the driver's side and let herself in.

The car smelled new, even though she had bought it used. It was stiflingly hot. She shoved the key into the ignition, and the car started immediately.

One hurdle down.

She rolled down all the windows, cranked the air, and sighed softly.

She had an emergency kit on the floor of the backseat—another change of clothes, a wig of short, curly red hair, makeup that had probably melted by now. She was tempted to grab the wig, but it was too different from her hairstyle now. Anyone watching the video later would wonder what happened to her hair.

Better to drive out like some local after a long trip. If she didn't do anything out of the ordinary, no one would notice her.

That was the theory, anyway.

Usually she used the extraordinary to hid her real motives. She'd never done things the traditional way before.

But she had no choice this time.

She pulled the crumpled piece of paper out of her purse and typed the address written on it into her GPS. Then she put the car into reverse, and eased out of the parking spot, getting out of here.

Finishing the plan.

One step at a time.

— 52 —

Cahill hadn't heard from Dirksen in nearly an hour. He hoped that meant the FBI had got him. Otherwise, Dirksen would've called, would've pulled another favor.

He hoped.

Cahill was sitting at his desk, going over the records from Storvick's phones. His home phone had only local calls, mostly to and from his wife's job. The cell, though, had a series of calls to different area codes. If he remembered his area codes, these were in sequence—like they'd be for someone who traveled by car.

Cahill took the list and walked over to the other computer in the department. This computer was old, buggy; a back-up, really. But Ingram was still using the good computer, trying to find more hits on the van, not that they needed them.

The case belonged to the Feebees now, and they could have it. Cahill would focus on Storvick, see if he could solve that crime, maybe bring something to the Feds.

Make him feel important, particularly after Dirksen reminded him of how dirty he'd been.

Dirksen would probably tell the FBI, hoping for a way out. Or maybe Dirksen had his own man inside.

Not that it mattered.

Cahill was clean now. He could say that with a straight face. He had led Dirksen on, got him arrested (he hoped), and saved his own ass. He hadn't taken any bribes—not here in Nevada—and there was no proof he had done anything wrong in California.

The LAPD had agreed to that when they decided to let him go. Mutually agreed. Cahill would leave with his experience and résumé, but no real recommendations (hell, anyone could see through that—anyone with a brain), and the LAPD would deep-six the file.

He hadn't been the kind of corrupt that made news. Nor had he been the kind of corrupt that was worth pursuing. He had been going in that direction, but he hadn't achieved it.

Too many others were that kind of corrupt. Too many to prosecute. Better to clear them out than pursue them.

Better to let him go than to pursue him.

He hoped.

He sat at the computer, wishing for the state-of-the-art crap he'd used in LA. Hell, smart phones were better than this thing. But he didn't have a smart phone, and he wasn't going to use his computer at home for police business.

So he sat down, took the list of numbers and typed them into a reverse directory in the order they appeared.

Then he mapped them.

Payphones, all along I-80.

The blond woman had been calling Storvick? That couldn't be possible. Why would she do that?

Cahill went back to his desk and called Storvick's cell provider. Cahill explained who he was, explained that he already had the list of calls (thank you very much), and explained that he needed one more thing.

"Any voice mail messages?" he asked.

"I have a note in the file that says we've send the text of them to your office," said the woman on the other end. She sounded official and disinterested at the same time.

"I'd like to hear them," Cahill said.

"I have two," she said. "From four days ago and two days ago."

"Can you play them for me?"

"We've sent the text—"

"I know," he said. "I want to hear the voice. In fact, send us the digital download with the text."

"I'm not sure I can do that, sir."

God, he hated rules and the idiots who followed them to the letter. "Just let me listen," he said.

The woman sighed, but she complied. In a minute, he heard the first voice mail message.

Sorry we missed each other, Gary. It's imperative that we speak. I need your account number.

And then the second voice mail message:

Sorry we missed each other, Gary. I need that information from you before I deposit the funds into your account. I'll call back in two days, between twelve and three. Talk to you then.

Neither message had been left by a woman.

"Do I have a list of which calls went to voice mail?" he asked the cell phone rep.

"Probably not," she said. "The first should be on your list for four days ago at 1:43 p.m."

He circled the call. It hadn't come from a pay phone.

"And the other from two days ago came in at 10:43 a.m."

Forty-three being the time in common. As well as the first six words. A code?

This call hadn't come from a pay phone either.

"Can I hear them again?" Cahill asked.

"I suppose," the woman said. She played them again. He listened closely, certain this time.

Not only were the voices not female, they weren't even from the same speaker. Two different men had called.

Cahill asked for the digital readouts again, thanked her, and then plugged the two numbers into the reverse directory.

The responses didn't surprise him.

The first had come from Lincoln, Nebraska. The home of the first murder victim on the day he died.

The second had come from Salt Lake City. The second murder victim on the day he died.

She'd had them do her dirty work. Cahill felt a moment of elation at that realization, followed by a wave of disappointment.

He would have to give this stuff to the Feds. He sighed.

It wasn't his case after all. Cahill had hoped that this murder was separate, like the murder in Tonopah. But it hadn't been.

And the woman hadn't been killing at random. She'd probably been slaughtering a child porn ring.

Who could argue with that?

Deep down, he knew he couldn't.

He shut down the computer, went back to his desk, and put the phone information in Storvick's files. Then he leaned back in his chair. For an afternoon, he'd thought he had a case.

But all he was going to be was the lackey for the Feds, instead of the lackey for Dirksen.

Nothing much for him to do.

He should've minded that more.

But, really, deep down, he didn't. He hadn't moved here for the excitement.

He'd moved here for the quiet.

And that was what he was going to enjoy, after all.

— 53 —

Moira pulled into the storage company.

It didn't look like Mecca.

Instead, hundreds of storage units glimmered tiredly in the bad lighting. The parking lot was hot because of all the metal around her. A sign on the way in had told her that each unit was "climate controlled," which meant that it was heated or cooled depending on the season.

Moira hadn't expected that.

Any more than she expected the storage unit to be here, just off I-15, heading to Los Angeles.

Somehow she'd expected the units to be closer to Nellis Air Force Base, but who flew money out of the country? It got shipped out. And Gary had told her, all those years ago, about the pain in the ass it had been to take the money and divide it between various storage units.

What an idiot Gary had been. A total damn fucking idiot. He wrote the information on a piece of paper to give to his contact. She hadn't even had to pull the information out of him before she shot him.

Good thing she saw that paper before she started grilling him. She'd been worried that he might fight her.

She leaned out of the car, tapped in the combination that opened the storage unit's gate. Then she drove in slowly, looking for the unit with the number he had marked.

Gary, the idiot, had made his first mistake the night he got drunk at the apartments in Wisconsin between tours. He told her about stealing millions of dollars from the government, dollars they didn't even know he had. Him and two other guys, who then split the money. They thought the money was marked, the dumb fucks. They sat on it, finally deciding to sell its location for a lot less than they'd have if they just spent it.

Dumb in so many ways. He had finally clammed up when she asked where the storage unit was. She'd thought he was making it all up, not that she cared. She was working another job. He was just a neighbor, part of her cover, someone who kept the suspicion off her.

It wasn't until that job was over that she decided to check his story. And to her great surprise, it checked out.

He'd been stupid, but not quite stupid enough to rent the storage unit in his own name. She checked every town he'd lived in, checked all kinds of databases, and never did find the unit.

She didn't even know how to get to the money until Kasey's job had come along.

When it did, Moira used another contact to hook up with Gary, never telling him who she was. She even used one of those voice disguisers when she initially talked to him, so that he thought his contact was a series of men, working for an unnamed boss.

She smiled to herself. It helped to have those guys she killed call Gary as their very last act.

Mintner, in Des Moines, had been very persuasive. He'd gotten Gary to admit that the storage unit was in Vegas, which relieved her. Even if Gary wouldn't tell her which unit or where, she had a finite area in which to search.

And then she'd arrived at his house, and there the information was, on a little piece of paper, so he wouldn't get it wrong after his contact transferred the money into his bank account.

Dumb fuck. He never suspected her. He wanted her out of the house so he could finish his deal.

Well, Gary had never been much in the brains department. It was some kind of miracle that he'd held onto the money this long.

She wanted to kiss Kasey for giving her the excuse to kill Gary. Moira had been waiting for a case like this one, something that tied a bunch of people together. Something that pointed in the exact wrong direction.

The authorities came late to the game, but they were here now. And they'd track her, ascribe motives she didn't really have (but she empathized with them. So nice to do a good deed while taking care of herself), and make all kinds of assumptions about her and her crimes.

She'd be in their database forever—or at least, the identity she discarded would.

She pulled up in front of the unit whose number was on the paper. The unit was even smaller than she thought it would be, smack in the middle of a row of units. She glanced at the combination lock and hoped it would open for her. She had another in the trunk along with a pair of bolt cutters, but she didn't want to go through the hassle of cutting the lock away.

She got out and grabbed the lock. It was still warm from the heat of the day. She slowly dialed in the combination, and the lock clicked open. Dumbass Gary, leaving a combo lock clearly provided by the storage company on this thing. Her breath caught.

She wasn't even sure the money would be here.

Someone else had probably taken it.

She grabbed the door handle and yanked the metal door open. It squealed in protest. Dust motes rose from the interior.

She could barely see in the lights the storage company had placed on each row. She squinted.

There, in the very back, was a pile of storage boxes. White file boxes, banker's boxes.

Her heart pounded.

She grabbed a tiny flashlight from her purse. Then she went inside and pulled the door down halfway so no one could see in. Then she opened one of the boxes.

Hundreds in groups of one hundred, bound together, four to a package, just like banks did it. She opened another box and then another.

Goddamn. The money was here.

It was amazing how small fifteen million dollars looked. Just some boxes in the back of a tiny storage unit. Unimportant, like someone's old photos.

She wanted to do a little dance. Fifteen million dollars in untraceable bills. Bills that everyone thought were lost in Baghdad.

She wouldn't take it all at once. That would be greedy.

Worse, it would be noticed.

Instead, she'd go to the trunk of her oh-so-practical sedan, remove the giant purse she'd had in there since she bought the car, and take a hundred grand or so. That would last her for a while.

Then she'd come back and dip in again.

First thing she'd do, though, was rent a different storage unit nearby. She'd move the boxes so that no one searching through Gary's things found this one. She'd probably have to do that tonight.

She'd keep everything in her new unit until she had a place of her own to store the boxes. That would take some thinking.

She wasn't used to having places of her own.

Sure was a lot she could do with this money.

She could retire. She could travel—and not for work. She wouldn't even have to go by car, if she didn't want to.

And she could occasionally dump some of it into a fund.

For Kasey.

Just in case Analyn screwed up.

Moira would be watching—especially since she'd have to come back to Nevada every few months or so.

Moira couldn't quite decide. Did she want one hundred grand per year? That didn't seem too greedy. Hell, she'd probably have trouble spending that, since she didn't like high-end clothes or fancy cars or even big houses.

She could even see herself getting restless. She was restless already.

Probably because she wasn't done.

She still had thirty million to find. Thirty million hidden somewhere by Gary's stupid friends.

She had their names. She could find out information about them, track them down.

Particularly if she had the right cover.

Maybe she'd keep working for Dealmakers after all.

When they had the right job.

Just like this one had been.

Be the first to know!

Just sign up for the Kristine Kathryn Rusch newsletter, and keep up with the latest news, releases and so much more—even the occasional giveaway.

To sign up, go to kristinekathrynrusch.com.

But wait! There's more. Sign up for the WMG Publishing newsletter, too, and get the latest news and releases from all of the WMG authors and lines, including Kristine Grayson, Kris Nelscott, Dean Wesley Smith, *Fiction River: An Original Anthology Magazine, Smith's Monthly,* and so much more.

Just go to wmgpublishing.com and click on Newsletter.

About the Author

USA Today bestselling author Kristine Kathryn Rusch writes in almost every genre. Generally, she uses her real name (Rusch) for most of her writing. Under that name, she publishes bestselling science fiction and fantasy, award-winning mysteries, acclaimed mainstream fiction, controversial nonfiction, and the occasional romance. Her novels have made bestseller lists around the world and her short fiction has appeared in eighteen best of the year collections. She has won more than twenty-five awards for her fiction, including the Hugo, *Le Prix Imaginales,* the *Asimov's* Readers Choice Award, and the *Ellery Queen Mystery Magazine* Readers Choice Award.

Publications from *The Chicago Tribune* to *Booklist* have included her Kris Nelscott mystery novels in their top-ten-best mystery novels of the year. The Nelscott books have received nominations for almost every award in the mystery field, including the best novel Edgar Award, and the Shamus Award.

To keep up with everything she does, go to kriswrites.com and sign up for her newsletter. To track her many pen names and series, see their individual websites (krisnelscott.com, kristinegrayson.com, krisdelake. com, retrievalartist.com, divingintothewreck.com). She lives and occasionally sleeps in Oregon.

www.ingramcontent.com/pod-product-compliance
Lightning Source LLC
Chambersburg PA
CBHW021032130626
46552CB00005B/1796